Granny Samurai

and the Brain of Ultimate Doomitude

John Chambers

WALKER
BOOKS

First published 2014 by Walker Books Ltd
87 Vauxhall Walk, London SE11 5HJ

2 4 6 8 10 9 7 5 3 1

Text and illustrations © 2014 John Chambers

The right of John Chambers to be identified as author and illustrator
of this work has been asserted by him in accordance with the
Copyright, Designs and Patents Act 1988

This book has been typeset in Brioso Pro

Printed and bound in Great Britain by Clays Ltd, St Ives plc

British Library Cataloguing in Publication Data:
a catalogue record for this book is available from the British Library

ISBN 978-1-4063-4105-8

www.walker.co.uk

For Dad

A Rainy Day

It was a terrifically dull morning and I was perusing a tome from my uncle's library.

This is the first sentence of a book I was thinking about reading. It was Friday after school and I was at home poking around in my Uncle Vesuvio's study. He had thousands of books in there, all neatly arranged, more even than the school library and better too, with better titles also. The school library has lots of books on sport, for example, to get boys reading who normally don't, which is a massive waste of time in my opinion.

This is because boys who are interested in sport prefer to do it instead of reading about it, while boys who aren't interested in sport don't like either. Therefore it is a double whammy, which means lose–lose, and the reason why I was in my uncle's study and perusing, which means reading bits out of, his books now.

My uncle, Lord Witherington Weatherby Willoughby, was a collector of fine volumes and valuable treatises pertaining to ancient matters.

This was the second sentence of the book, and excessively vital for luring the reader into reading the rest. My own uncle says that a good first sentence is like a fly dropped on the water to get the fish's attention. A good second sentence is the hook that snags the fish. The rest of the book is the angler reeling the reader in. These are metaphors, or mind pictures,

hello!

8

for explaining ideas – something my uncle is incredibly good at. I perused further.

What ancient matters this tome of my exalted relation would thus pertain to would thereof be demonstrated shortly and I prepared to roll my eyeballs over the coming paragraph.

I emitted a massive yawn and put the book back. I would rather read three books on sport than *that*. I pulled out another volume and looked at it. GREAT GOLF GAMES OF THE 1920s WITH PUTTING ILLUSTRATIONS. Well maybe not.

I returned the book to the shelf, and as I did, a page fell out of its middle. I bent down to pick it up. Drawings of golf courses, I thought, glancing down at the flimsy paper. What a massively dull and rainy day it was turning out to be.

Then I looked closer.
The page, only slightly
wider than my
hand, had
been torn from
an old notebook.
In spidery writing
on one side I could
just make out these
words: *Your Most Serene
Excellency, I have not long
now. The fire is dying and
I can hear their teeth rattling in the darkness.
The crew, oh heavens, the crew... I cannot write
it! Forgive me, Your Grace. I have failed you.
But what I have discovered is contained in these
few pages. Should they find you...*

As you can see, the "you" ended in a
squiggle, as if the writer's hand had slipped.
I enjoy scribing myself, as a hobby, and like
clean copy – which means no squiggles.

10

I wondered what had happened to make this writer's hand slip. I flipped the page over and studied the other side. There was a drawing of something on it, though not a golf course. It had been done with the same scratchy pen, like a nib that you dip into ink. I knew about this because of my scribal inks collection, which is quite large, though I mostly do my schoolwork on a laptop now. But in ancient times, everybody wrote with these pens. Everybody who could write, I mean. In ye olden times not everybody *could* write – or read, for that matter.

I examined the page again. The paper was excessively old and wrinkly and I wondered whose teeth were rattling in the darkness. The only person I knew whose teeth rattled was excessively old and wrinkly also, but her teeth rattled because they were false and she enjoyed the sound. Then I wondered where the other "few pages" were and spent the remains of the day in the library looking for them. Sadly, although I found a great many other interesting books, the torn-out pages I was seeking stayed sought. But by then the rain had stopped and the day was nearly over and had turned out pretty interesting after all. So that was good.

Here is a list of the top five interesting books I found in my uncle's study that day:

1. LOST WORLDS AND THEIR SUSPECTED LOCATIONS, WITH MAPS AND SHIPPING TIMETABLES. As this tome was printed in 1782, which is pretty pre-histrionic, I suspected they weren't that lost any more.

2. YOUR HOME IS YOUR CASTLE, WITH PRACTICAL ILLUSTRATIONS FOR BUILDING A MOAT, INSTALLING ARROW SLITS AND CONVERTING YOUR FRONT DOOR TO A DRAWBRIDGE. I admire drawbridges and considered proposing to

my Uncle Vesuvio that we build one.

3. WINNING THROUGH HYPNOSIS: SEVEN STEPS TOWARDS BENDING YOUR OPPONENT TO YOUR WILL. This is maybe

a bit too much like cheating, but it might be useful if your opponent is cheating.

4. SERIOUSLY TOP SECRETS. This book was printed in invisible ink and you had to iron each page to make the writing visible.

5. 100 AMAZING CHOCOLATE RECIPES. I decided to make recipe number 17 for tea.

Tea

This is me in the kitchen, making Amazing Chocolate Recipe number 17. It is called Chocolate Chicken Supreme. The recipe is: *Melt some chocolate. Draw the outline of a chicken onto a cold plate. Carefully pour chocolate into the outline. Let it cool. Eat.*

I ate.

While I was eating I studied the mysterious page again. The drawing was covered in funny writing, which I couldn't read. At least I thought it was writing. If you look at the picture of the drawing you will see what I mean. The truth is, I didn't know which way was up, or down, or even sideways.

My mobile rang and it was my Uncle Vesuvio. He told me to get my own tea as he would be home later than anticipated. I told him I already had.

"Well done, Samuel," he said, and hung up.

My uncle is a diplomat so it is second nature for him to be polite. It is also second nature for him to be delayed if there is a crisis somewhere. Which there generally is.

I finished my chocolate chicken and washed it down with an extra-chocolate milkshake. Then I committed the washing up. As I sudsed I went back to thinking about the page. Who was the Most Serene Excellency? I wondered. Whoever they were, they couldn't have been very serene after they read *that* note.

Outside the kitchen window darkness
was incoming, but at least there were no teeth
chattering. I decided I would show the page to
my uncle in the morning to see what he made
of it. Then I perused some more Amazing
Chocolate recipes for a while before leaving
the page in the book as a
bookmark. After that I
went to bed. That was
Friday.

Saturday

Early Saturday morning
I woke to the sound of the
front door closing behind
my uncle as he left for
the office. He must have come
home late, while I was asleep.
"A diplomatic crisis is like a pot
burning," he says, "and I am a fireman."

    I went downstairs and there was
a note on the table. *Dear Samuel*, he had
scribed. *I will be back late
tonight, tomorrow at the latest.
Your uncle, V.* I frowned slightly
at this, as the last time he had left a note
like that, the next time I had seen him was a
week later being crushed in the gizzards of a
giant boa constrictor*. But as tomorrow was
my birthday, I was assured that he would do
his best to be there. My birthday is always
important to my Uncle Vesuvio.

* See *Granny Samurai,
the Monkey King and I.*

Breakfast

I put some milk on to
heat while I fetched
the newspaper and
simultaneously pondered which chocolate
recipe to make for breakfast. Usually I do
the easy crossword while my uncle reads
the cartoons, which are always best on
Saturdays. Then we swap and he does the hard
one. We both have scribal natures but he is
more advanced than me because he is older.
Sometimes our neighbour Granny Samurai
comes over to join us and does the Sudoku
as well. This can be distracting, however,
as she clacks her teeth loudly when she is
concentrating – and even louder if
you ask her politely to stop.
Also, she is an impatient
person, which is not
good for doing
Sudoku.

Here is a joke about teeth. It is from my favourite comic strip ever and is most revolting.

HORRID + UGG by Jo Zimmer

HEY UGG, WHY ARE YOU LICKING YOUR VICTIM?	I CAN'T FIND MY DENSHURES.	WELL WHY DON'T YOU JUST GET NEW ONES?	I DON'T MIND IT MAKES MY FOOD LASTS LONGER.

I was looking forward to this cartoon now as I bent down to extract the newspaper from my letter box. Then the newspaper was extracted from my hand instead. I frowned and opened the door.

The garden was empty. Surprise!

0016094y

A Horrid Ambush

Actually it wasn't really that surprising.
I surmised swiftly that a certain somebody
had grown impatient waiting for her Sudoku
and had taken the newspaper into her own
hands. With one hundred per cent precision
I knew who that somebody was. Granny
Samurai! I leant over the railing between
our houses and rang her doorbell. She didn't
answer. Oh come on, Granny, I thought, and

reached up to bang on her door with the heavy iron knocker.

"AHHH!" it shouted in a loud electronic voice when I lifted the ring. "Leggo by dose!"

Ha ha, hilarious, I thought, and knocked loudly while the stupid thing's eyes flashed bright red and purple. That is just the kind of thing Granny Samurai finds excessively amusing. But there was still no answer. I frowned in ponderment. Then something pinged me hard on the back of my neck. I looked around and caught a glimpse of someone small and vile watching me through the bushes near the front gate. The gate itself was ajar and half my newspaper fluttered beneath it.

"Hey!" I said, as a prelivery to uttering something else, then a hail of yellow and orange pellets peppered into my mouth and stopped me.

"Ack ack ack," I coughed, and spat a yellow pellet out into my hand. It was a small, hard, plastic ball – sort of like a Tic Tac, only much less delicious.

A second blast flew at me like tracer bullets. Near the gate the someone small and vile had mutated into two someones small and vile. From the street outside, two small ugly boys were firing at me with their toy guns. Meanwhile, just inside my gate a small ugly dog was panting horribly and doing an unspeakably large something right on top of what was left of my newspaper.

The unspeakable something was nearly as big as he was and part of my brain wondered how this could be possible. Another part, however, was causing me to boil over and advance sternly towards the invaders, ready to repel. But as I strode forth, a third part was going, *sniff sniff*, and I suddenly realized I wasn't the only thing boiling over.

"The milk!" I shouted in alarm and turned and ran back into the house. There in the kitchen the milk had risen at top speed to the rim of the saucepan and beyond. Now it was burning vigorously on the stove and ponging up the place most awfully. By the time I had cleaned it up, and the garden too, and rescued what bits of newspaper I could, the evil twins had vanished and my breakfast was completely and entirely ruined.

I spent the rest of the morning failing to do the hard crossword, which was the only part of the rescued newspaper that didn't smell. Then I tried to scribe a bit in my diary, but couldn't. Finally I just gave up and watched TV instead. On the nature channel there was a programme about giant Amazonian meat-eating plants, which was most informative. Maybe, I thought, I could get one for the garden. For beside the gate.

Shop 'Til You Drop

In the afternoon I went shopping. As it was my birthday the following day I intended to buy the ingredients for my best cake ever – or at least up until now. Recipe number 12 from 100 AMAZING CHOCOLATE RECIPES sounded excessively delicious to me. It was called Molten Volcano Chocolate Fudge Surprise.

Personally I prefer cake mix to cake, but my uncle said that maybe we could do half and half this year as some people quite like to eat cake as opposed to drinking it. Him, for example. As I quite like my uncle also, I agreed that I would do some baking as well as mixing. Therefore it was a good omen to discover the Molten Volcano Chocolate Fudge Surprise recipe, which combined the best of both. You bake it, but when you cut into it, it erupts in molten chocolate fury. SURPRISE!

I wrote out my shopping list and exited the front door. The curtains in Granny Samurai's house were still drawn and I desisted from knocking in case she actually *was* sleeping. Sometimes she stays up all night watching television and sleeps during the day.

"Isn't that a massive waste of time?" I once asked politely.

"Not if you like television," she replied. I was considering this when an unexpected unpleasantness occurred.

There Goes the Neighbourhood

My gate was blocked.
A huge cardboard
box had been
dumped right
outside it –
and in case
I might have
been able
to squeeze

past, another one had been placed in front
of that. Nice, I thought – and thanks! – and
wondered who had put it there. I soon found
out, as a hail of yellow and orange pellets
assailed me. It was the evil twins again.

"Gottim!" shouted one.

"No, I gottim!" shouted the other, and
then they started firing at each other instead.

At least it isn't personal, I thought, then
ducked as they turned and fired at me again.
Or maybe it was.

Behind them, a huge removal van was parked, and a man who looked like a grown-up version of his evil offsprigs spake into one of two mobile phones, completely ignoring what they were doing.

"You're not listening," he was saying. "You're not LISTENING."

"Excuse me," I uttered, but he wasn't listening, either. "Excuse me," I tried again. "I can't get out of my gate."

"YOU'RE NOT LISTENING!" the man screamed into his phone again, then he broke off as the other one rang. "WHAT?" he shouted. "NO! I'M BUSY! GO AWAY!" He hung up and went back to the first one. "YOU'RE STILL NOT LISTENING!" he shouted.

I looked up and down the street. It was littered with hideous gold furniture and cardboard boxes everywhere, and the horrible dog from earlier was busily chewing a hole in one so that a blizzard of white Styrofoam packing beads was whirling around the street and making a giant mess. The twins, meanwhile, were now firing pellets at the movers whilst a thin woman shouted, "DON'T YOU DARE DROP THAT BOX!" and "OH, GOOD SHOT, JULIAN!" and "I DO THINK IT IS IMPORTANT THAT BOYS EXPRESS THEMSELVES, DON'T YOU?"

"Excuse me," I shouted, and waved, trying to get her attention.

"OH LOOK, BOYS," she screamed, "THERE'S A LOVELY LITTLE BOY OVER THERE FOR YOU TO PLAY WITH! HELLO, LITTLE BOY!" And she waved back.

The evil twins swivelled their evil eyes towards me again and I emitted defeat. For the second time that day.

Victory and Defeat

My uncle says that in life there is the Long Game and the Short Game. Sometimes you have to emit defeat in the short game so you can survive for the long game. Granny Samurai calls this Using Defeat.

"Use how?" I asked her once.

"Use dem to run away," she snorted.

"Hee hee hee." And she slapped her wooden leg in hilarity.

Hee hee hee, I thought irritably as I used mine to retreat back into the house, through the kitchen and over the wall into the back lane behind. If those people were moving in next door, this could turn out to be a very long game indeed.

Lists

This is my shopping list for the cake:

1 large jar of golden syrup
5 medium bars of dark chocolate
1 large bar of white chocolate
1 kilo of flour
6 eggs
1 kilo of sugar
vanilla essence

When I noticed that three large bars of chocolate cost less than five medium ones (with more chocolate in total), I bought the three large ones instead. I saved some money *and* had extra chocolate to munch on the way home. This was a win–win situation and highly yum.

The Way Home

Here's me, walking home eating chocolate. My mobile rang and it was my friend Philip, who was coming tomorrow and wanted to check what time, even though I'd texted him twice already, duh!

"Oh … right," he said, and hung up.

Philip is my best friend from school but I had invited others from our class as well, including Meegan, whom I now sat beside. Boris, who is a thug I used to have the not-pleasure of sitting beside, wasn't coming, because he wasn't invited. In fact he stays well away from me these days, which is excessively fine by me.

My phone rang again and I answered it with automatism, saying, "Why don't you just check your texts, you muppet."

"Oh," said my Uncle Vesuvio, "I must have missed one."

"Whoops!" I said. "I thought you were Philip." And then I saw my uncle. He was up ahead of me in the street, about to turn the corner into our road. "Wait," I said, pretending, "I will now telepathically guess where you are. You are just about to turn the corner near our house."

Instead my uncle turned around and smiled at me. As a diplomat he is trained to see "all the angles", therefore he is a hard man to trick. He waited for me to catch up and we turned the corner together. This is what we saw.

Chaos.

Chaos

"Chaos," says Granny Samurai, "is."

"Is what?" I asked, as she had uttered this mini-wisdom whilst dictating to me her as-yet-unfinished "masterpiece", THE LOST SECRET ART OF KENJO.

"Chaos is," she replied.

"Is what?" I said again.

"Open brain box listen," she barked. "Chaos IS!"

"You mean chaos *exists*?" I asked carefully.

"I mean *everything* is chaos," she replied, "and chaos is *everything*. Order for ninnies. Chaos? Sit back enjoy relax. Order big fat headache to go."

Everything Is Chaos

"Goodness," uttered my uncle, surveying the aftermath of the new neighbours' move – though actually it was anything but. As far as the eye could see (to the end of Summerhill Road) the ground was strewn with white Styro bits, shredded cardboard boxes and rubbish all-sorts. Two large cars were parked outside our house and Granny Samurai's. The pavement was covered in yellow and orange pellets.

"Tic Tacs?" enquisited my uncle, raising one eyebrow.

"Bullets," I replied darkly. Then I explained what had been happening in his absence.

"I see," he said, frowning. Then he frowned even more as we came to our gate and I heard a familiar panting noise from just inside the garden. I will spare the sensitive reader a picture of what we beheld. All I will say is, that little dog must have a digestive system like a combine harvester.

"Goodness," said my uncle again. "Goodness gracious."

Then it started to rain yellow and orange pellets. Somehow I wasn't surprised.

A Note on Neighbours

In cold northern climes like Scandinavia people don't like their neighbours very much. Once I read a story about two Vikings who lived on opposite hills to each other. Every day one shouted a message across to the other but the other was so far away it was hard for him to hear. Finally he understood. The message was: Go away!

This would be a good message for our new neighbours, I thought, even though we weren't living on a mountain, or in cold northern climes either.

I imagined shouting it at them through a megaphone: GO AWAY! But then I imagined the answer coming right back at me: I'M NOT LISTENING. So I stopped imagining and waited to see my uncle swing into full diplomatic action. Sometimes it is good to have a grown-up present. This is how the conversation went.

The Art of Diplomacy, Starring Uncle Vesuvio (UV) and Nasty Neighbour (NN)

UV: Excuse me, but your dog is messing up our garden path.

NN: Hello Peter, it's George. Let me call you right back.

UV: Excuse me, I said, Your dog is messing up our garden path.

NN: Two minutes, all right?

UV: *Excuse me...*

NN: Yes?

UV: I *said...*

NN: You don't have to shout, you know. I can hear you perfectly well.

UV: I wasn't shouting.

NN: So I'm lying, is that it? ARE YOU ACCUSING ME OF LYING?

UV: Your dog. HAS messed up. Our garden path.

NN: *[Pause.]* Well, you shouldn't have left your gate open.

UV: I didn't leave the gate open.

NN: *[Pointing at me.]* Maybe *he* left it open!

Me: I wasn't *able* to open it, because it was blocked.

NN: Well, whatever. Just leave it closed in future, all right? Hello Peter, it's George again.

And turning around, he recommenced his conversation with Peter, whoever that was. My Uncle Vesuvio gave his back a stern look.

UV: And what about the mess?
NN: Hang on, Peter. *[To Uncle Vesuvio.]* It's your garden, *mate*. You clean it up.
UV: It's *your* mess.
NN: Well now it's yours.
UV: I'm asking you for the last time…
NN: I'M NOT LISTENING. I'M NOT LISTENING.

And with that, the neighbour turned back to his mobile phone and plugged the other ear with one finger while his evil offsprigs leered in our direction.

PLUG!

NN: No, not you, Peter. I'm listening to *you*.

The twins smirked while my uncle took a deep calming breath. Although he says that a good diplomat never loses his temper, I could see by the back of his neck that he was supremely tempted. I wondered what his next move would be. I never found out.

Why I Never Found Out

Because a loud horn blast interrupted everything, including our neighbour's telephone conversation. We all turned around and gaped – which means stared in amazement – as a massive truck steered slowly into our street and rumbled towards us. The engine growled like a warthog with indigestion and the yellow and orange pellets vibrated on the ground like bouncing hail. The truck was huge and black and square, with tinted windows and chugging chrome pipes. The tyres were thick and ridged. On its side was a vigorous airbrush painting of a tiger battling a dragon against the poetic backdrop of a full moon whilst dolphins soared out of the mystic seas beneath. With a seismic hiss of brakes the truck shuddered to a stop just outside our gate and the horn blared once more. Then the engine ceased its rumble and a tinted window hummed downwards. The evil twins turned pale and their horrible dog yelped and ran into the hedge to hide.

The only sound to be heard in the sudden silence was our awful neighbour saying, "Peter, I'll call you right back."

Then Granny Samurai stared out through the passenger window and looked him dead in the eye. "You're in my parking space," she growled.

Tigers vs Dragons

This is an excessively ancient motif from parts of olde Asia. The tiger symbolizes strength and the dragon symbolizes cleverness. Sages of the era used to ponder philosophically who would win in an ultimate battle, the tiger or the dragon. My friend Philip, who is a modern sage, often ponders who would win between Batman and Superman. I believe Superman would win because only kryptonite can defeat him – which does not exist on Planet Earth. Granny Samurai says she would bet on Batman because he would cheat if he had to, whereas Superman wouldn't.

"But cheating isn't winning," said Philip.

To which Granny replied, "Duh! Of course not. Winning is winning." And she cracked her thumb knuckle to emphasize the point.

Now she glowered down at our neighbour from the driver's seat of her truck and the neighbour scowled back. My uncle looked at me and smiled ever so slightly.

"I believe," he said, "I will leave this confrontation to Henrietta while I go inside and put the kettle on for tea."

And he did. Both, I mean.

Tea vs Coffee

My uncle's favourite tea is Earl Grey.

I like regular tea with milk in it. Granny Samurai only drinks cold instant coffee. When she hasn't had any for a while she can get quite cranky. This is what flashed through my mind as I watched her staring down the neighbour. To give him his due, he stared back evilly. At least until his staring was interrupted by his wife.

"GEORGE!" she screamed. "GEORGE, WHAT'S TAKING YOU SO LONG? JULIAN, DICK? WHERE ARE YOU? WHERE IS YOUR FATHER? OH, HELLO AGAIN, LITTLE BOY! [*i.e. Me!*] OH, THERE YOU ARE, GHENGHIS LAMB! [*The dog.*] WHY ARE YOU HIDING IN THE HEDGE? GEORGE! GEORGE? WHO IS THIS STRANGE PERSON YOU ARE STARING AT AND WHY IS SHE BLOCKING OUR ROAD?"

The last question was addressed to Granny Samurai but via George, which is an annoying habit some grown-ups have.

Granny Samurai growled, "I'm waiting for my parking space to open up."

"WHAT PARKING SPACE?" screamed George's wife,

whatever her name was. I still hadn't found out.

"MY parking space," said Granny Samurai. "And that's the last time I'm going to say it."

"THAT'S A DISABLED PARKING SPACE!" screamed the woman. "ONLY DISABLED PEOPLE CAN PARK THERE."

"Assuming they can drive," muttered George with an unpleasant smirk, "haw haw haw," and their unpleasant boys smirked also.

Granny Samurai leant further out of the window and pointed her stick at him. Her stick conceals a Black Centurion double-action repeater, of which there are only two in the world. But she was just pointing it of course.

"Are you disabled?" she asked coldly.

"OF COURSE NOT," screamed George's wife while George smirked again most horribly. I was beginning to wonder if he had any other facial grimaces.

"Well, *I* am," said Granny Samurai, "and that's my parking space. And unless you move your car by the time I count to five, I'm going to take my wooden leg and do a jig on your car from bonnet to boot that will leave it looking like a junker that got dumped there by a tornado. And after THAT," she uttered, starting up the engine with a mighty roar, "I'm going to park there ANYWAY."

"How dare you!" spluttered George, but the tinted window was already sliding up.

"I'm not listening," burbled Granny as she disappeared from view. Then she revved the engine again and blasted the horn once for good measure as the twins and Ghengis the dog ran for the safety of their garden. George moved his car.

That was Saturday.

Happy Birthday to Me

On Sunday I got up early to bake my birthday cake. My uncle says nobody should have to work on their birthday, but baking is not work because I enjoy it greatly. Also, I am a better baker than my uncle so this is a win–win situation for all. I was in the kitchen getting the ingredients ready when Granny Samurai appeared suddenly behind me. Chapter seven of THE LOST SECRET ART OF KENJO reveals how to do this, and even though I now know how, I still nearly always get a heart attack when she commits it.

"Aahh," I gasped, fumbling 100 Amazing Chocolate Recipes so that my shopping list fell from it. With a quick pinching movement Granny Samurai caught it in one hand. In the other she clutched an old instant coffee tin with holes punched in the lid and sellotape wrapped around it.

"Interesting," grunted Granny, glimpsing at my list most closely. "Multo-interesting." Then she glimpsed at me most closely instead. "Where you get this, Sam?" she asked.

"I wrote it," I replied politely, wondering what was so multo-interesting about a shopping list, especially as Granny has no interest in baking. She stared at me so hard I blinked and looked away, which is a very natural reaction to being stared at by Granny Samurai. I looked at the page in her hand instead.

"Wait!" I emitted with sudden realization. "That's not my shopping list. That's a strange piece of paper I found in Uncle Vesuvio's study yesterday."

"What strange piece of paper?" asked my uncle, entering the kitchen with a large wrapped parcel under his arm. Then he prevented me from answering his own question. "Wait, Samuel," he said, "first things first." And he looked at Granny Samurai, who grinned, and they both opened their mouths and started singing – one tunefully, one loudly (guess which one, ha ha) –

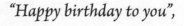

"Happy birthday to you",
and when they were
finished, he held
out his parcel and
she held out her
tin and I took
them both with
happy anticipation.

I enjoy birthdays, especially my own,
and am highly interested in presents. Multo-
interested, actually.

Presents

Presents are very excellent, both to give and
receive. As a diplomat my uncle is ultra-adept
at giving presents, and wrapping them also.
For example mine was wrapped in special
hiroglyphic paper from the ancient Egyptian
section of the British Museum.

Hiroglyphics are thus called because the
ancient Egyptians used to hire scribes to

write their glyphs for them, which is a way of saying letters. As a scribe myself, I am quite interested in all this, which is how my uncle knew I would like the paper.

I unwrapped his parcel and inside was a globe of the world with internal light settings so that you could watch the sunrise spreading around the world at any time of year – and the seasons too, or even the world lighting up

at night. Also it was an alarm clock. It was excessively spectacular and I had had my eye on it for some time.

"Wow," I said. "Thanks, Uncle Vesuvio," and gave him a hug. "It's borker." Then I turned to Granny Samurai's tin. It was old and battered, with **HBS** scrawled on the side in thick black letters.

"HBS?" I quizzled, and Granny rolled her eyes turbulently. "Happy Birthday, Samuel?" I guessed.

She patted me on the head and grunted ironically, "Duh, hello brain." Then she rubbed her hands together as if she was making fire and added, "But what's inside, Sam never guess ever."

I studied the holes in the lid. Whatever it was, it needed to breathe.

"Henrietta," spake my uncle doubtfully, but Granny held up one finger in warning.

"Shh, V," she said. "It doesn't like being woken."

"Woken?" I said, with slight intrepidation.

"Woken!" said Granny, grinning.

"Err ... thanks," I replied, and gazed a second longer at the tin. Then I girded my

lions and, in one quick movement, peeled
the lid off and looked inside.

"Empty," I said, and Granny grabbed the
tin and peered inside herself.

"Oh, yabba!" she uttered,
and stared
wildly around
the kitchen as
if hunting for
something.
"That's not good."
"What's not
good specifically?"
I asked, but my question petered
out in mid-air. Granny was gone as suddenly
as she had arrived (see chapter nineteen
of THE LOST SECRET ART OF KENJO), and
because her disappearance was so sudden,
neither my uncle nor I noticed that she had
taken with her the page with the mysterious
writing on it.

A Garden Party

This is my back garden. As you can see I have set up an outdoors table for my birthday party. Granny Samurai lives on one side of us and she is invited. The horrible new neighbours live on the other and they are not, of course.

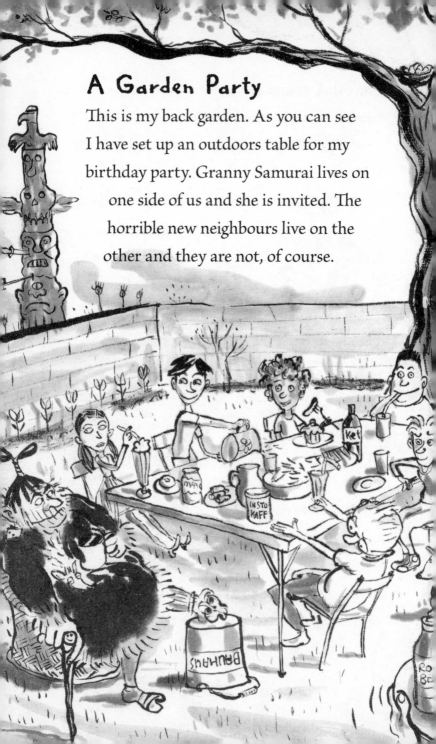

The other guests are:

1. **Philip Sydney** (my best friend from school)
2. **Meegan Flowers** (also from school)
3. **David Curley** (also in my class)
4. **Maximilian Leonard** (known as "Gonks")
5. **Michael Finn** (an exchange student from Ireland who has brought his dog Wowser with him)

My Uncle Vesuvio is coming and going, serving us delicacies such as crisps (three different flavours), Coke, Sprite and juice (two different kinds), sausage rolls (Wowser especially likes these), cold instant coffee (for Granny Samurai), no-crust sandwiches with salad cream, and homemade chips – which taste nearly as good as the ones from the chipper – with salt and vinegar and ketchup, and mayonnaise for Meegan (who likes mayonnaise on her chips because her mother is French). The birthday cake is on a separate table and I am keeping that for last. It is the "crowning glory". Now, however, we are sitting together and making polite conversation. This is Philip's idea of polite conversation.

Polite Conversation, Starring Philip Sydney

Philip: So, like, how did you lose your leg?

Meegan: Philip!!!

Granny: Who?

Philip: Er ... you?

Granny: Me what?

Philip: How did you lose your leg?

I didn't bother to interject – which means interrupt – because Granny Samurai is bulletproof when it comes to "polite conversation", as you will see.

Granny: What leg?

Philip: Er ... that leg.
[Pointing at wooden leg.]

Granny: Leg still here.

And she banged her wooden stump hard with her stick and squished some cold instant coffee around her gums while Philip frowned and thought about his next question.

Philip: But that leg's wooden!

Granny: So?

Philip: So what happened to the other leg?

Granny: Other leg still here, look.

And she twitched up her skirt to
show a glimpse of stockinged leg
and what might have been a tattoo.
Philip tried again.

Philip: I mean, what happened to your leg
before it was a wooden one?

Granny: I suppose it was a tree.

Meegan: *Mmpff!*

That was the noise made by Meegan
as she sneezed into her chips while
trying not to laugh. Some landed
on the ground beside Wowser,
who barked loudly (*Woof!*) and
pounced.

"Wowser loves chips," announced Michael Finn. "My da' says he should have been a chipmunk."

"Chips are the only vegetable I ever eat," said Gonks solemnly. "Ever!"

"Very wise," said Granny Samurai and slurped some more coffee. "But ketchup is a vegetable too," she added.

Gonks looked surprised. As a fervent – which means passionate – disliker of vegetables he was uncomfortable with the thought that he was eating more than he realized. Meanwhile, Philip was still holding forth upon his current favourite topic.

Philip: What I mean is, you only have one leg, right?

Granny: One left. One right. Same as you.

Philip: But only one is real. Correct?

Granny: Leg number one: real mahogany. Leg number two: real Brazilian ironwood. Leg number three: real titanium. Also real.

She banged her non-false leg with her hand.

Michael Finn: I think your leg is deadly.

Granny: Which one?

Meegan: *Mpppff!*

Wowser: *Woof, woof!*

My birthday was turning into the Mad Hatter's tea party. Then it got worse.

How It Got Worse

It started raining yellow and orange pellets.

"What on earth...?" said Meegan, picking the pellets out of her hair.

"Hic," said Gonks, swallowing one and turning sort of yellow himself.

"Ouch," ejected David Curley as one hit him in the eye.

Only Philip turned to look where they were coming from. "There!" he said, pointing as the pellets bounced off his glasses.

"Brattage in tree next door. Burn it down," suggested Granny calmly. The pellets didn't seem to bother her at all.

"Let's just ignore them," I replied, "and they'll get tired of their stupid game and go away." Granny snorted loudly and Philip looked at me doubtfully.

"You think?" he said.

"I do," I said firmly, "and it's my birthday."

Granny made a noise like a balloon flying around a room and Meegan looked at her in alarm. "Is she laughing," she asked me, "or having a heart attack?"

But before I could answer, the rain of pellets ceased.

"See," I said. "It works." Then Wowser barked and his ears went straight up like antennae. We turned to look at what he had seen. With diabolical quietude the small horrible dog from next door had wormed his way into my garden and sneaked right up on my birthday cake. Now he was about to take a giant bite out of it. Vindictive mirth came from the twins in their tree. The pellets had only been a diversion.

Molten Volcano Chocolate Fudge Surprise

The alert reader will recall that although this is a baked cake, when you cut into it, it erupts in "molten chocolate fury". Biting will work also. Surprise!

Here is a picture of the rotten dog running at top speed out of our garden.

His rotten owner would have to give him at least three baths to get the golden syrup out of his fur, and it served them both right.

"Wow," said Michael Finn. "I need that recipe for my brother's next birthday."

"Brilliant," said Philip. "Totally genius, Sam."

"Juice, anybody?" said my uncle, emerging from the kitchen. And: "Did I just miss something?"

The Rest of the Party

The rest of the party passed in ultimate peacitude. We even rescued some of the cake and ate it. Meegan gave me a present of a scarf, which I put on and she said looked pretty good. This was quite pleasant as she was the one who had given it to me. Gonks gave me a book about an animal called the Amazing Olm that lives on a waterfall in a dark cave in Slovakia – which is in deepest Europe – and is completely blind.

"Er … wow," I said politely, although I privately wondered why that was amazing and not just odd. Possibly "amazing" sounded better.

Michael Finn gave me a family pack of crisps from Ireland called Tayto, which he said are the best crisps ever because they are full of preservatives. They were in fact supremely excellent.

Lastly, Philip presented me with a pen and moleskin notebook. "Brilliant," he said, "for scribing in." Which is what I like to do. "Something interesting," he added unnecessarily, "for prosperity." (Which means later.)

And then they all sang "Happy Birthday" again, except for Granny Samurai, who had fallen asleep and was snoring so loudly that Wowser pressed his ears shut with his paws. And thus at long last my party was over and the guests went home – apart from Philip, who was staying over due to it being a bank holiday the following day. We planned on going to a new climbing centre that had just opened, and doing some climbing.

"Like Spider-Man," said Philip, brushing his teeth before we retired for the night. Then he wondered between brushes who would win in a fight between Batman and Spider-Man.

I said, "That won't work because they inhabit parallel universi." (This is the plural of universe.) "Technically, therefore, they can never *actually* meet."

"Right," said Philip, spitting into the sink. "I forgot that." Then he recommenced holding forth, i.e. banging on, about Granny Samurai's leg. I brushed my own teeth and stared out through the bathroom window at her house next door. There was a full moon in the sky and one light on upstairs.

Probably she was sitting up watching television. That is one of the nice things about being a grown-up, you can do what you want, even if it is bad for you.

"You don't think she's pretending, do you?" asked Philip later, from the mattress on the floor beside my bed.

"Pretending what?" I enquisited.

"I mean, what if her leg is just curled up under her dress?" he said.

"Philip," I said in a seriously non-polite tone, "shut it." And he did. For a while, anyway.

The Witching Hour

Here is my house, 5 Summerhill Road. It is the witching hour (which means the middle of the night, which actually means ultra-early in the morning). My uncle is asleep and I am asleep and Philip is awake. He has just woken up because he has heard a little noise in the darkness and wants to share this information with me. Thanks, Philip.

This is how the conversation went.

Philip: [Whispering.] *Sam, wake up. Wake up. I can hear something.*

Me: What?

Philip: *There's something in the room with us.*

Me: I can't hear anything.

Philip: *Shh ... listen. There. Did you hear it?*

I did hear it. I sat up in bed and listened. It was a kind of soft flat *flump*, like a flummy sack being dropped on a wooden floor. I heard it again. It sounded weird, and weird in the middle of the night is generally not good.

Philip: *It's coming from the landing. Maybe you should go and see what it is.*
Me: Why don't YOU go and see what it is?
Philip: *Because it's your house. And I'm the guest.*
Me: *All right. Let's both go.*

Sometimes it is good to have somebody staying over and sleeping in the same room as you.

This is us, peeping out the door.
We saw ... nothing.

74

We looked closer.

Nothing except the light under the door of my uncle's study.

"My uncle must be working late," I whispered. "That must be what we heard." I confess I was somewhat relieved. Then Philip clutched my arm and pointed to a dark corner of the landing.

"Look," he hissed. I looked. By now my eyes had adjusted to the light. This is what I saw.

It could have been a hamster, but it hopped like a frog. (That was the flummy sound we heard.) And it could have been a frog but it was hairy like a hamster, with eyes as big and pale as Smarties with the colour sucked off. As we watched, it opened a mouth full of surprisingly spiky teeth and let out a high-pitched ribbitty howl. Then it turned and forced its way under the study door. Its hind legs kicked and ripped the carpet *en passant*.

"What *is* that thing?" emitted Philip nervously, and I said, "Come on, we'd better warn my uncle." Thus, seizing a convenient tennis racquet and a cricket bat we advanced towards his study.

I was just about to fling the door open when a voice I knew snapped from inside, "Come in Sam. Quick quick. Close door behind you."

What We Found

Inside, Granny Samurai was standing amidst a rubble of books. In one hand she held her battered coffee tin and with the other she was sellotaping the lid back on again.

"Was that *thing* my present?" I uttered in sudden realization.

"Happy Birthday to you." She grinned and thrust the tin at me.

Ooowww!

I took it cautiously and it jumped in my hands as the thing tried to get out. A small howl drifted through the holes.

"Hold tight," snapped Granny. "Lucky to catch before."

"Before what?" asked Philip.

"Before next birthday," cackled Granny. "Goodbye."

She turned to go but I uttered, "Wait! What happened to the study?"

Uncle Vesuvio is as orderly as I am, but now his books lay thrown around the floor as if somebody had been searching them for something.

Granny Samurai looked pious and shrugged. "Frog mess books maybe?" she suggested.

"What frog?" said Philip. "Oh, you mean the *thing*. Is that really a frog? Are you sure?"

I looked pointedly at Granny and questioned, "Why exactly would a *frog* be interested in *books*?"

"Hello, said MAYBE," snapped Granny. "Maybe yes maybe no.

Anyway, goodbye!" She rattled her teeth at me and turned to defenestrate – which means exit by the window. But the teeth-rattling jogged my brain and I suddenly knew exactly what she was up to. Frog indeed! I reached into my memory and quoted:

> "The fire is dying and I can hear their
> teeth rattling in the darkness. The crew,
> oh heavens, the crew... I cannot write it!
> Forgive me, Your Grace. I have failed you.
> But what I have discovered is contained
> in these few pages."

As a scribe I have a superlative memory for the written word, even if those words are scribbled on an old torn page. Granny turned swiftly and gave me a hard look. So did Philip.

"He's gone mad," said Philip, almost to himself. "Poor Sam has lost it."

I held out my hand to Granny. "Give it back," I said, but she just frowned.

"I meant *lost it* as in *bonkers*," said Philip, "not like actually losing something."

Granny ignored him and reached into her coat. Slowly she pulled out the flimsy piece of paper. On one side I could make out the tiny scrawl and on the other, the drawing with the strange words.

"And the other pages?" I said.

"Not here," shrugged Granny. "Looked looked long time, not found."

She handed over the page.

"Hey, cool," said Philip, gazing at it as I took it in my hand. "Mirror writing!" Both Granny and I turned to stare at him. "Isn't that obvious?" he said.

What Philip Saw

On page 16 the alert reader can refresh his memory of what the drawing looked like when I first saw it and compare it to what Philip saw now. And in case you are thinking it was stupid of us not to have noticed – well, did you? As for Philip, he is mostly wrong about everything, but when he is right, he is mega-right. Like now.

I pondered the drawing. But only for a second. Then Granny Samurai grabbed it out of my hands and defenestrated swiftly.

"Goodbye and goodnight," she cackled.

The Uses of Scribing: A Practical Demonstration

In ancient times scribes were trained to learn thousands of poems and massive oral epics by heart. I only had to remember one. At top speed I sprinted to my bedroom and seized the moleskin notebook Philip had presented to me for my birthday. Using my full scribal abilities I sketched down everything I could remember from studying the drawing.

"Wow," said Philip, who had followed me into the bedroom and was giving me the thumbs-up. "Nice one, Sam." I held the notebook up to the bedroom mirror. This is what we saw: *E Pluribus Universum*.

"That's Latin," quoth Philip. "It means, er ... something pluribus universe."

I said, "It means one universe among many."

"Really?" said Philip. "Are you sure?"

Philip is rubbish at Latin but I enjoy it – not only because of its superior precision factor but also because so many words come from it that we still use today, like precision

 or rubbish. Philip says you can't even say "hi" in Latin, just stuff about "ye gods" and Julius Caesar, but I believe this is missing the point. I looked at the mirror and read on.

"*Inkibus minkibus succubus omnibus. Poopla hoopla moopla.* That last part's not Latin," I said. "That's something else."

"Really?" said Philip. "Are you sure?"

"I'm sure," I replied. When it comes to languages, Philip can't tell a cuckoo from a chainsaw.

I spake the sentence again. "*Inkibus minkibus succubus omnibus. Poopla hoopla moopla.*"

Philip frowned and leant forward. "Look," he said, but I had seen it too.

In the middle of the reflection in the mirror, a hole was opening up. It looked exactly like when you burn a piece of paper with a magnifying glass.

"The page is on fire!" emitted Philip in astonishment. Except it wasn't. It just looked like that in the reflection. He reached out to touch the mirror and the words started glowing fiercely as his hand approached. "Wow," he said, and read the words out loud. *"Inkibus minkibus succubus omnibus. Poopla hoopla moop—"*

"STOP!" I shouted suddenly, but I was too late.

"—*la*," finished Philip, at the same second as his finger touched the glass. With a sound like a Mister Slush being slurped through a straw, Philip vanished into the mirror. He didn't even have time to look surprised. But I did. I know this because I could see my own face above the hole, now closing, staring back at me in shock and horror.

Spells

I don't like spells. Spells disrupt the natural order of things.

"Well *duh*," said Granny Samurai when I shared this thought with her once. "That's what spells are for."

"But that's why I don't like them," I persisted.

Granny snorted loudly and gave one of her eyeballs a good scratch. "What natural order?" she grunted. See "Chaos" (page 37).

SOS!

Gripping my notebook tightly, I sprinted towards my uncle's bedroom. As a diplomat he has much practice at emergencies, and I needed him right now. I jerked open his door and stopped. His bed was empty. His pyjamas were folded and his slippers neatly aligned. It was the middle of the night and he was gone. There must have been a crisis somewhere. I grabbed my mobile and rang him.

"You have reached…" began his voice in dulcet tones. I hung up without leaving a message. My uncle would see who it was and call me back ASAP. He always

called me back ASAP.
I looked out through the
bedroom window. The
street lights were still on
but I could see that the
dawn was coming. In
Granny Samurai's upper
back window a light flickered
like a signal. I pulled on my
jacket and ran downstairs to the back
door. I needed help quickly, and so did Philip.
I needed a grown-up. I jumped over the wall
and let myself into her kitchen.

"Granny Samurai!" I shouted, stepping
onto the welcome
mat. The mat fell
away from under
my feet. Like Alice
in Wonderland,
I plunged straight
after it.

Traps

Chapter forty-nine of THE LOST SECRET ART OF KENJO, as dictated by Granny Samurai, deals with traps. The chapter is titled "Gotcha!"

Traps, writes Granny Samurai, *are second only to a good ambush for fun and hilarity.*

I hesitated in my scribing. "Why second?" I asked.

"Because the personal touch is absent," she explained.

"What personal touch?" I said.

She grinned and closed her hand into a solid-looking lump. "The swift knock on the conker," she elaborated. "The headlock mightily applied. A trap is an ambush on remote control. Ambush no sleep. Stay awake. Good trap sleep sweet big dream big."

Gotcha!

I wasn't sleeping now. Or dreaming, for that matter. Instead, I stood in a hole in Granny Samurai's kitchen and shouted for her to come and pull me out. The mat was in the hole with me and scratched my shins excessively. On one side was printed WELCOME and on the other, NOT.

The walls of the hole were polished smooth and higher than I could jump. If she hadn't come home  after defenestrating with the drawing then I was in big trouble.

If she had decided to go away for a bit of a holiday I was in even bigger trouble.

"GRANNY SAMURAI!" I roared again. "Heeeeelllllp!"

A second later
her head appeared
above me.

"Hee hee
hee," she
cackled loudly.
"Hello Sam."

"Philip's
gone!" I shouted.
"He got sucked
into the
mirror."

Granny frowned in puzzlement.
"How?" she asked. "Granny pinched –
whoops, *borrowed!* –
drawing back."

"I made a copy,"
I shouted, "quick
quick." Her pithy
style of talking was
quite contagious.

Now Granny frowned
even harder. "Copy quick
quick brain thick not
quick silly Sam stick to
scribing thank you."
And she turned to go.

"WAIT!" I shouted. "WHERE
YOU GO? I MEAN, WHERE *ARE* YOU
GOING?"

Granny reappeared and stared down at
me irritably. "What you think? Get Fred back
before too late."

"I'm coming too," I said and Granny shook
her head.

"Too dangerous. Sam stay here instead.
Goodbye."

"BUT," I screamed, "if it's too dangerous
and you don't come back, I'll starve to death
down here!"

Granny thought about this for a moment.
Then she clacked her teeth in annoyance,

93

and reaching down she grabbed me tightly by the hair and hauled me up into the kitchen.

"Ouch!" I said loudly.

"You're welcome," she retorted, and shoved me out the door before her.

"And his name is Philip, not Fred," I added.

"Whatever," Granny snorted rudely. "Let's go."

We went.

A Bump in the Night

Back in my house, the hallway was dark and my seven senses told me that something inside was badly wrong. Nevertheless I remembered how when I was small my Uncle Vesuvio used to sit me on his lap and recite the following rhyme:

Things that go bump in the night
May give you a terrible fright.
But don't lose your head,
Or hide in your bed,
Just reach out
and switch on the light.

On "light" he would open his
knees and let me fall through.
I thought of this advice, and the falling feeling
also, as I clicked the switch and nothing
happened. "That's odd," I spake nervously, as
the bulb was new.

Granny Samurai ignored the oddness
and shoved on past me up the stairs. By the
weak light of dawn I could see her wooden
leg pounding dust out of the carpet. That was
odd too – I distinctly
remembered hoovering
before the party.
I coughed and followed.

95

Yoo hoo!

At the top
of the stairs the
oddness increased.
The skylight barely lit
and I saw that the pane
was thickly covered with a
horrible mat of spiders' webs.
It looked as if a clutter of spiders
had been busily weaving there
for aeons. Yuck, I thought, and
wondered how I had missed cleaning
that – or getting Uncle Vesuvio to
do it. Although intellectually I know
that I am much bigger than spiders, I am
still quite uneasy around them.
Philip thinks that spiders
are cool. A web brushed
against my hair and I
recoiled in horror, trying
to wipe it off and only
making it worse, of course.

"Stop wriggling," hissed Granny, and yanked me towards my bedroom door. "I'll go first," she ordered. I didn't argue.

On the Dark Side

A light came on. It shone from a small and powerful Maglite Granny had gripped between her molars. She adjusted the beam and pushed my bedroom door open with her stick. The door creaked with an ancient squeak and I thought, since when does my door squeak? I peeped around her, then stopped thinking and gaped instead.

My room was an ultimate mess.
My books were yellow and
old. The covers on the
bed were faded. The
carpet was full of holes

and looked like moths had been
busy raising entire families there
for generations. And everything,
from ceiling to floor, was covered
with a thick, dense layer of dust.

Granny stepped inside and swung her head from side to side like a cobra. Her eyes glinted and she ignored the moths that fluttered around her mouth, attracted by the Maglite. I hoped she didn't inhale any – for the moths' sake, I mean. Then a sound made me twitch.

"Philip?" I said semi-hopefully. "Is that you?" From a corner of my room the hairy hamfrog stared balefully at me from a rusty coffee tin. Only now it looked different. Its hairs were sparse and thin, its skin wrinkled like a collapsed balloon. It opened its mouth to howl and I could see that half its teeth were missing. I thought it looked tired and old.

Until I saw myself in the mirror. Then
I learnt what tired and old looked like.

It looked like me.

Self-Portrait of the Scribe as a Young Boy

This is me in
the mirror.
It must be a
trick of light
and shadow,
I thought with
horror. Then
I thought,
if I, as
a young
person,
look like this,
what does Granny
Samurai look like? I turned my eyes to gaze.
The mirror exploded.

This is Granny Samurai, who has just
fired a single shot from her Black Centurion
double-action repeater. The mirror shatters
then immediately starts repairing itself.
The repair looks like ice crystals
melting and
is excessively
unnerving.

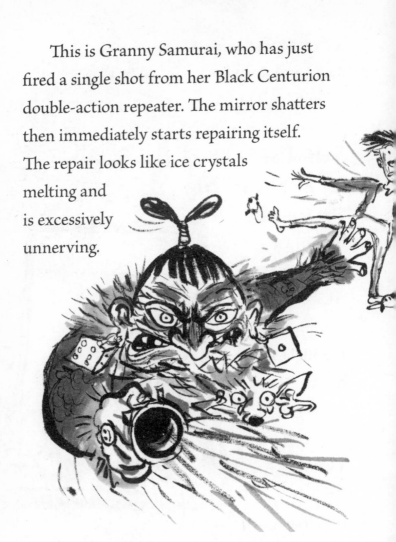

I stared wildly at Granny. It looked
like she was melting also. As I watched, her
wrinkles grew wrinkles and her hair turned

frizzy. Only her eyes
and teeth stayed
bright. My brain
screamed at me
to leave the
room ASAP
but my body
didn't respond.
Granny reached for my arm and shoved me
towards the window.

"No," I croaked, sensing what she had in
mind.

"Yes," she mumbled, kicking the window
open with her foot. I tried to prise her hand
from my collar and failed.
"Brace brace," she muttered,
and let herself topple.
Her steely grip dragged
me after her. We
defenestrated into
the bush below.

This is me,
landing.

This is Granny,
hobbling through the garden at medium
speed and dragging me along
behind her.

HOBBLE... LIMP...

Here she is,
"helping me" over the
hedge near the gate.

The hedge was overgrown and needed clipping. I landed with a thump on the street outside.

But the weird thing was, the further away I got from my house, the better I felt. I picked myself up and looked back in horror. The window to my bedroom was cracked and broken,  the plaster around it falling off in lumps.

The window looked like it belonged in an abandoned house. A loud *chirp* interrupted my thoughts and the lights on Granny Samurai's truck blinked on.

105

"Get in," she snapped and started up the engine. There was a huge growl and the lights on the neighbour's car went on as well. He had parked it too close, of course.

An annoying electronic voice spake: STEP AWAY FROM THIS CAR NOW. I climbed over the bumper and got into her truck.

Granny revved the engine and I looked back at my house again. A rot had spread from my bedroom window, and the roses, in their beds below, were wilting and dying.

"The roses!" I emitted in horror. My Uncle Vesuvio was quite fond of his roses. With one hand Granny threw the truck in gear and with the other she spun the steering wheel and released the handbrake. In front of us our neighbour's SUV was shunted rudely off to one side.

"Whoops," cackled Granny, and pressed her wooden leg down hard on the accelerator. The engine roared like an angry hippopotamus and I was shoved back into my seat as the truck charged forward into the dawn.

That's us. Gone.

Speed Trap

We drove towards town. Granny Samurai pulled out her iPod and scrolled quickly through it.

"WHERE ARE WE GOING?" I shouted, trying to be heard above the roaring engine.

Granny glanced at me and shouted back, "NEED BIG MIRROR."

I screamed in return, "THERE'S A FULL-LENGTH MIRROR IN MY UNCLE'S BEDROOM!"

"BIGGER," bellowed Granny. "MUCH BIGGER!"

"HOW MUCH BIGGER?" I roared.

"MULTO-BIGGER!" she boomed and slotted her iPod into the dashboard. "Turkish Song of the Damned" by the Pogues started pouring from the loudspeakers.

"*I come, old friend from hell tonight,*" they sang as Granny sped even faster. Behind us a blue light commenced whirling and a loud siren wailed.

"IT'S THE POLICE!" I shouted. "THERE MUST BE AN EMERGENCY SOMEWHERE." Granny glanced quickly in the mirror then changed gear with a blurring motion. The engine growled like a charging buffalo and the truck went faster.

I uttered, "SHOULDN'T WE LET THEM PASS AQAP?" AQAP is an abbreviation I invented and means AS QUICKLY AS POSSIBLE. Uncle Vesuvio says you should always let the emergency services pass AQAP. Granny Samurai ignored me, and the siren. Behind us a second blue light joined the first one and an angry voice shouted through a loudspeaker: "YOU IN THE TRUCK, PULL OVER IMMEDIATELY."

I suddenly realized that the emergency was us. "Oh crim," I aghasted. "We're in trouble now."

Granny shifted up a gear. "Wrong," she grunted. "We're in a hurry."

WHOOOHHH
WHOO...

We sped towards the centre of town.
Thankfully the streets were deserted on
account of the early hour and there was
nobody to run over at high speed. My
stomach flipped like a pancake as the truck
swung left onto the main street and my side
rose high into the air. I strongly prefer not to
be driving on two wheels when I can avoid it.

"TAKE DRAWING QUICK!" screamed Granny, banging her fist on the roof in time to the music.

With a thwobble (thump plus wobble) the truck slammed back down onto four wheels.

"HOLD IT UP TO WINDSCREEN!" shouted Granny next.

I held it up to windscreen.

It is quite hard to argue with Granny Samurai in full ordering mode. Behind us the police were shouting through their loudspeakers. "PULL OVER. YOU. ARE. UNDER. ARREST!"

Great, I thought unhappily. I had never been arrested before and I suspected that my uncle wouldn't be too pleased about it either. We turned the wrong way into a one-way street and my attention was distracted by a swiftly approaching office building at the other end. In fact, the office building *was* the end of the street. Trapped in a cul-de-sac, we were now at the mercy of the pursuing constables.

Granny Samurai commenced mumbling. *"Inkibus minkibus succubus omnibus. Poopla hoopla moopla."* I looked askance at her – which means in disbelief. The office building was appoaching fast. *"Inkibus minkibus succubus omnibus. Poopla hoopla moopla,"* she said again, louder this time, as behind us the police cars skidded to a screeching stop. Wasn't it time for us to do the same? *"INKIBUS MINKIBUS SUCCUBUS OMNIBUS. POOPLA HOOPLA MOOPLA!"* roared Granny as, too late, the building loomed. I could see my horrified face in its mirrored facade. It looked pale.

Through the Looking-Glass

In ye olden days a mirror was called a "looking-glass". This was because it was made of glass and you looked at it and that was about all you did. Now I was not only looking, I was about to crash into one, which was a most unpleasant prospect. The "multo-bigger" mirror that Granny had meant was fourteen storeys high and otherwise known as the prestige headquarters of the International Bank of BizCom Ltd. I could see myself clearly in its reflection, holding up the strange drawing and approaching at about a million miles an hour. Behind us the police sirens were writhing and I was wassailing

114

as my ultimate doom did dawn. Then, in the last second possible, a giant hole opened up in the mirrored cliff before me. Its edges looked like they'd been scorched by an enormous magnifying glass. If I hadn't been so engaged in terror and panic, I might have considered turning around to behold the expressions on the faces of the constables behind us. It would have been worth a gaze, however brief, for, with a noise like an elephant slurping an entire swimming pool of Mister Slush through his nose, we drove into the hole and it closed up tight behind us.

Goodbye, world, I thought. It was nice knowing you.

SLURP

Mysterious Holes

According to our science teacher, Mr Dardis Corbet, there is quite probably more than just the one universe in which we dwell. Mr Corbet is tall and thin with a voice that could zonk a zombie.

"You mean like parallel universes, sir?" said Philip when the teacher first brought up the subject.

To which Mr Corbet replied, "*Universi, Mr Sydney, universi.*"

Mr Corbet also teaches Latin.

"Yes, sir, right, sir," replied Philip, "parallel universi. Like Spider-Man and Batman, which is why they can never meet."

"Er … correct," said Mr Corbet, surprised that Philip was taking an interest in science.

"Unless, sir, they went through a wormhole," added Philip, surprising him even more. "Then they might meet."

Gonks said, "You know, in an emergency, you can eat worms."

"Eeeeww," said Meegan. "That's disgusting."

Mr Corbet knocked on the table for silence, which is something he always does.

"Come in," said David Curley in a low voice, which is something *he* always does, and we all laughed.

"Silence," said Mr Corbet. "Now, Mr Sydney, for ten points, maybe you can tell us exactly what a wormhole is."

"A wormhole," answered Philip, "is a portal between two univers—i. It is usually caused by a warp or fold in space–time and must be kept closed at all times to prevent the forces of ultimate doomitude from invading us. Because if the forces of ultimate doomitude invade us, we'll all be destroy—"

"Thank you, Mr Sydney," interrupted Mr Corbet. "You were doing quite well up until the last bit."

"You're welcome, sir," said Philip. "Shall I continue?"

"No," said Mr Corbet, "definitely not."

This was all stuff I thought about later, by the way. It is not what I was thinking as we drove through the hole into somewhere I knew not where. At that moment I was too preoccupied with screaming.

Inside the Hole

Here is a picture of
what it looked like
falling into the hole.
As you can see,
the hole doesn't
seem to have any
sides, so how,
you might ask,
can it be a hole?
The answer is,
I don't know, but
it certainly started
as a hole. Also, if
you look closely at the
picture we appear to be
falling weightlessly, but
why would you fall if you are
weightless? All in all it is a great
anomaly and certainly worthy of
further investigation. Just not by me.

120

Arrival in the Great Unknown

And then we arrived. In an instant we were weightful again and brought back down to earth by the forces of gravity. At least I hoped it was earth.

"Grrraaannuugghhh," I started to yell in high alarm – that is how "Granny" comes out when the truck thumps to a sudden stop and you are nearly choked by your seat belt. The paper fluttered out of my fingers and back

into hers. Through
the windscreen
I could see a snowy
landscape and perceived that we
had landed in a drift. Except the snow was
grey, not white, and made me think of ashes
not flakes.

Was this where Philip was? But where
was *this*, exactly? On the other side of
the International Bank of BizCom Ltd
was normally a pleasing public park. This
place was as pleasing as a post-apocalyptic
Antarctic. I shook my head vigorously – it
was full of scrambled thoughts and I needed
to order them. Maybe some fresh air would
help. I wound down the window and took a
deep breath. Big mistake. The fresh air that
came in was about as fresh
as Philip's socks. I closed
the window again quickly.
If everywhere here smelt

like that then Philip would feel right at home,
but I was still worried about him. As a child
I'd moved around considerably and Philip
was the first best friend I'd ever had. I was
determined to find him ag—

A sudden knock on the head interrupted
my thoughts and nearly made me bite my
tongue.

"Ding dong ding dong!" shouted Granny.
"Hello hello anybody home?"

I rubbed my head and said stiffly,
"You could have just *said* my name instead
of hitting me."

"Hello SAM!" shouted
Granny. "Wakey wakey please.
Shout Sam Sam SAM
three times loud Louder
LOUDEST.

What happen, big fat nothing what. Lost in daydream what. Socks, Fred, friend. Boo hoo hoo."

"It's rude to read people's thoughts," I said, annoyed at her prying.

"Then pay attention," she snorted. "Now. Truck stuck. Sam out. Give truck push big now! Granny steer."

I emitted a hollow laugh. "Push the truck?" I said. "You want me to *push the truck*?"

"Blah blah blah," emitted Granny back to me. "Whatever. You steer I push."

And she did.

There was a mighty bump and the truck lurched forward.

She hopped back in and seized the wheel again. "Let's go Joe," she muttered, and pressed play on her iPod again. "Like Meatloaf?" she asked. "Singer not food."

"No and no," I replied honestly.

"Too bad," she snorted.

This is us, driving through the Great Unknown. You can't hear it but we are loudly playing "Bat Out of Hell" by Meatloaf. Or at least Granny is. And singing along, which is worse. I can reliably report that even though the ride was short it seemed incredibly long.

A Note on Meatloaf

Meatloaf is a singer from the
Rock Age who got his name
because he once allowed
a Beetle (the car,
not the insect)
to drive over his
head. Granny
Samurai says
Meatloaf is a "classic"
and she has all his albums. Uncle Vesuvio
defines a classic as anything that has been
around long enough for its value to become
apparent. A well-made chair, for example.

BUMP!

Philip Sydney has a collection of classic comics that his mother keeps trying to throw out. For example, he has issues one, two and four of *Tales of Decay*, a story in four parts. Sometimes he has arguments with his mother about them, where he says, "Have you any idea how much these comics are worth?" Then she says, "Tell me and I'll pay you double to get rid of them."

Philip has never won an argument with his mother yet, but he keeps trying.

Personally, I am more attracted to books than comics. Philip thinks it should be illegal to publish books without pictures. He is my best friend but we disagree on most things. Somehow that doesn't bother me.

Off-Road Driving

We drove off-road. Or maybe there just was no road, I wasn't sure. The ashy landscape all around revealed no edges I could see. I looked at my mobile phone. It was blinking and asking me if I wanted to reset everything NOW. The crash must have damaged something, I thought. We drove and drove. Two renditions of "*Bat Out of Hell*" later, Granny swerved sharply and the truck started jiggling like a washing machine. Now we really were off-road.

129

Outside, the landscape turned jagged and all of a sudden dropped away like my jaw as the truck slowed down and squealed to a stop. We had arrived at a coast somewhere, a horrible rocky coast with high dark cliffs and a sea below, the colour of milky porridge. A long flat bridge extended all the way out into a distant swirling mist. And through the mist a baleful smudge shone. I supposed it must have been the sun. Granny Samurai reached down and switched off the music. Thank goodness, I thought privately, then immediately changed my mind. The wind outside sounded like a thousand ghosts with toothache. It buffeted the truck and stirred up the awful sea below.

"There," said Granny, and pointed. "That's where
we're going."

"Into the mist?" I spake nervously and she gave me a look. Being given a look by Granny Samurai is like being poked in the ear by anybody else.

"Oh Granny please please please take me with you please please," she minced.

I replied, annoyed, "I'm just *asking*. I haven't changed my mind, you know."

"Good," she said, then grinned. "Don't worry Sam. Boring part over. Fun start soon." I must have blanched a bit. "More Meatloaf?" she requested. I nodded palely.

More Meatloaf

This is us,
driving onto
the bridge at full-tilt,
playing Meatloaf at top volume. I am
singing along loudly, trying to drown out my
thoughts. It's not working.

My Thoughts
Here is a picture of
my thoughts at this
time, to illustrate how
it is not working.

Crossing the Bridge

The bridge was dark and rusty and drooped in the middle like an aged clothesline. It didn't look especially stable and I started to ponder exactly how much the truck weighed. At some point Granny switched off the music and the headlights too. Considering the bridge had no railings, I wondered if this was wise – but suspected I knew the reason why. Granny Samurai was always big on the element of surprise.

Up ahead the mist abated and I perceived our destination. It was an island, emerging from the surrounding fog. It was large and dark and pointy and pickled with craters and holes. In its middle was a large cave, into which the bridge entered. It reminded me

most uneasily of a gaping mouth. Beyond
it, the sky was an appalling putty colour.
I glanced at Granny with supreme nervosity.

"What is this place?" I uttered. But
instead of answering she hauled most fiercely
on the brakes and the truck slewed and
slowed. A small red light had appeared on
the bridge before us. "A cyclist?" I opined
hopefully, keen for some sign of normality,
but Granny snorted loudly. The red light
dipped then lifted. I saw it was a lantern being
held by somebody.

"Hey, Sam," said
a voice I knew.

"Philip!" I answered
in astonishment[2].
"Is that you?"

135

Some Facts About Philip Sydney

Perhaps I shouldn't have been astonished. The fact is that Philip has a talent for showing up in places where he is not supposed to be. For example, he first joined our school by accident. (He was supposed to go to the one down the road.) However, by the time anyone noticed (including  him) he had grown to like it and decided to stay. And when he was born, it was in the taxi on the way to the hospital and not in the hospital itself.

"Which wasn't my fault," said Philip.

To which his mother replied, "It never is."

Now here he was again, standing on a bridge of weirdness, wavering a red light on a pole and looking at us most cheerfully. But at least he was there.

I opened the door of the truck and shouted, "COME ON, PHILIP, JUMP IN!"

"Greetings," said Philip, and didn't.

"HURRY UP, YOU MUPPET!" I shouted again, and he didn't do that either. I turned to Granny Samurai.

"Maybe his feet are stuck?" I queried, but she was busy ignoring me completely. (Granny Samurai's powers of ignoring are very considerable.) And while

she was ignoring me she was giving Philip her Max Power Stare. The Max Power Stare is the ability to magnify distant objects up to ten times 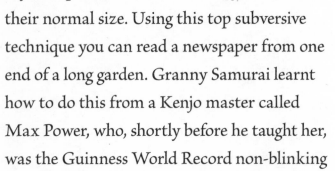 their normal size. Using this top subversive technique you can read a newspaper from one end of a long garden. Granny Samurai learnt how to do this from a Kenjo master called Max Power, who, shortly before he taught her, was the Guinness World Record non-blinking champion. Now the current champion, i.e. Granny, was sitting beside me, focusing her beadies on my best friend and frowning hard.

IF YOU CAN READ THIS FINE PRINT YOU STILL ARE'NT CLOSE ENOUGH.

"Not Fred," she said suddenly.

"Ha ha, very funny," I replied with exclusive irony. "And his name is Philip, by the way."

"FredPhilipPhilipFred who cares not him no sir no madam no way," muttered Granny, still giving him her top MPS.

Rubbish! I thought, but I looked hard all the same. Where Granny Samurai is involved, it is always better to look twice. Philip was now raising his red lantern slowly so that it pointed straight at us. "It *is* Philip," I insisted, and placed a foot outside the door as a prelivery to going to seize him instead of discussing eternally.

Granny Samurai shot out her hand and seized me instead. "I is wrong," she persisted, still not blinking.

"I know you are," I replied.

"EYES wrong," she barked. "Look close. Left eye green right eye blue. See?"

"Hello, I know that," I said sarcastically,

referring to the interesting fact that Philip
has eyes of different colours. "But that's not
wrong," I pointed out. "It's just unusual."

"Hello yourself, Fred *left* eye blue *right* eye
green. That's not Fred," growled Granny and
started up the engine. "Not annoying enough
either," she added as she stamped hard on
the accelerator.

The truck surged
forward, sucking
me back into
my seat.
"Sto-opp!"
I screamed,
but she
accelerated
instead.
Right at my
best friend.

How I Met Philip

I met Philip in the school library, where I was perusing a book in peace and quiet and he arrived and disturbed it.

"What are you reading?" he asked, and I lifted the book to show him. It was called THE DECLINE AND FALL OF ABSOLUTELY EVERYTHING and was a volume about disasters. "Are there pictures?" said Philip, and there were. We had embarked on a philosophical disco on the nature of disasters when the door opened and the headmaster walked in.

"You. New boy," he spake, and pointed at Philip. "Aren't you supposed. To be. Somewhere. Else?"

"Oh ... right, sir," said Philip. "Maths, I think." And he exited quickly.

"And what. Are you. Doing. Jensen?" added the head.

"*Johnson*, sir. And I'm reading, sir," I answered, which was pretty obvious, I thought (but didn't say) as I had a massive book open in front of me.

"Very. Good," spake the headmaster. "Carry on. Reading." Which I did. And that was how I met Philip.

Now I was sitting in a speeding truck and about to squash him flatter than a hedgehog on the M4. It was a very unenjoyable feeling.

A Quick Note on Hedgehogs

I admire hedgehogs. They eat slugs when nobody else will and can roll themselves into balls of ultimate protection. Sadly this doesn't work too well against cars, though possibly one day hedgehogs will evolve stronger hedges and correct the balance of nature. Unless of course they happen to meet Granny Samurai in her truck. Then even hedges of steel won't help.

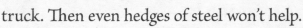

Accident-in-Waiting

We bore down on Philip. I would now like to ask the reader to imagine a large truck bearing down on you at high speed. At the very least you would faint, or dive to one side or start praying to ye gods or *something*. But instead of any of the above Philip merely smiled, then raised the red lantern high above his head and swiped it down hard. Just before we ran him over. I closed my eyes in horror.

Then opened them again. In the rearview mirror I could see Philip arise and watch us driving away. He wasn't squashed at all. In fact he just looked sort of fuzzy, as if he was made of bubbles and somebody had given him a good shake. Now the bubbles were bubbling back together and his lantern was gleaming so fiercely red I had to squint to behold it. Behind him on the bridge, a huge hole with glowing edges had opened up where he had whacked it. Then I noticed a thin glowing line slicing straight through the middle of Granny's truck.

"Oh yabba," grunted Granny, and grimaced. The truck split in two.

Sliced Loaf

Here's us, still going! There's the truck,
split neatly into two halves. As you can see,
Granny Samurai is perched in one and I am
in the other. We are like two slices of the same
loaf. On her side Granny Samurai is gripping
the steering wheel in vain, as it no longer
steers. On my side I am gripping my seat in
vain, as I don't know what else to do.

Meanwhile, all kinds of hi- and low-tech
weapons are tumbling out of the truck
onto the bridge behind.

With a curse Granny swivelled in her
chair, staring grimly back at her rapidly
scattering weapons of choice, then at
me. I had the highly uncomfortable
idea she was deciding which to save.

My side of the truck commenced
veering towards the edge of
the bridge. Other ideas
panicked my brain
instead.

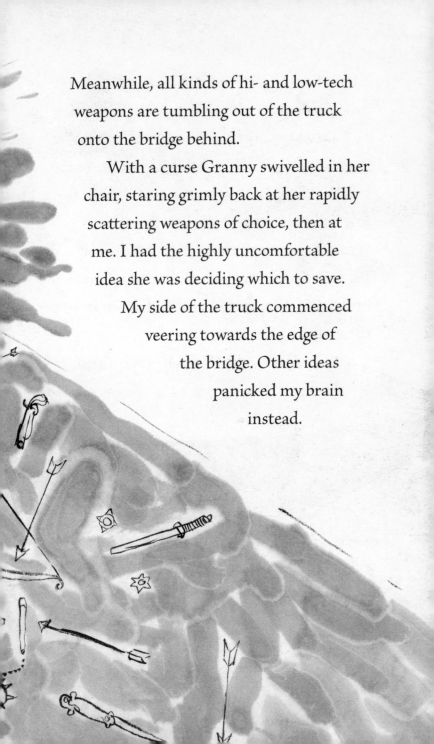

"Brace Sam brace!" shouted Granny, prodding hard with her stick to set me back on course. It worked. Sort of! With a metallic crashendo my truck-side toppled to the road and skidded like an oyster in a half-shell (me being the oyster) all the way towards the bridge end and the cave that did await. Behind me, Granny's truck-half veered off-bridge and plummeted over and down into the churning sea below.

"GRANNY SAMURAI!" I screamed,

150

and for just one nanosecond caught
a glimpse of a diamond-tipped claw
slashing through the air, aiming for
the bridge and missing by a whisky.
"NOOOO!" I shouted, sliding
decisively into the gaping cave
and darkness and arriving with
a screeching crash in the last
place in the world I really
wanted to be, especially alone.
Blackout and yabba!

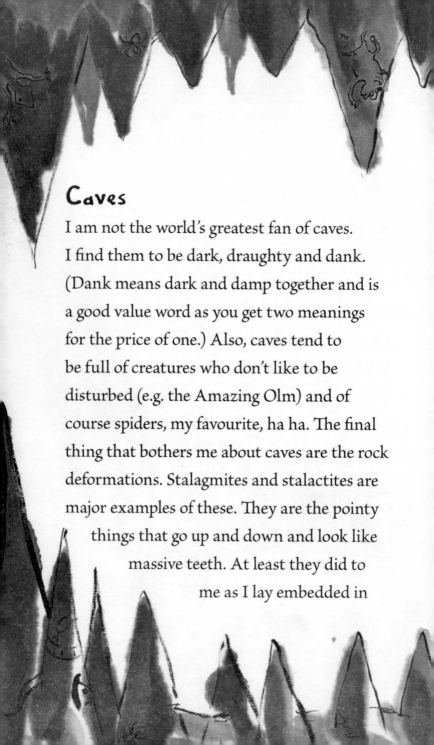

Caves

I am not the world's greatest fan of caves. I find them to be dark, draughty and dank. (Dank means dark and damp together and is a good value word as you get two meanings for the price of one.) Also, caves tend to be full of creatures who don't like to be disturbed (e.g. the Amazing Olm) and of course spiders, my favourite, ha ha. The final thing that bothers me about caves are the rock deformations. Stalagmites and stalactites are major examples of these. They are the pointy things that go up and down and look like massive teeth. At least they did to me as I lay embedded in

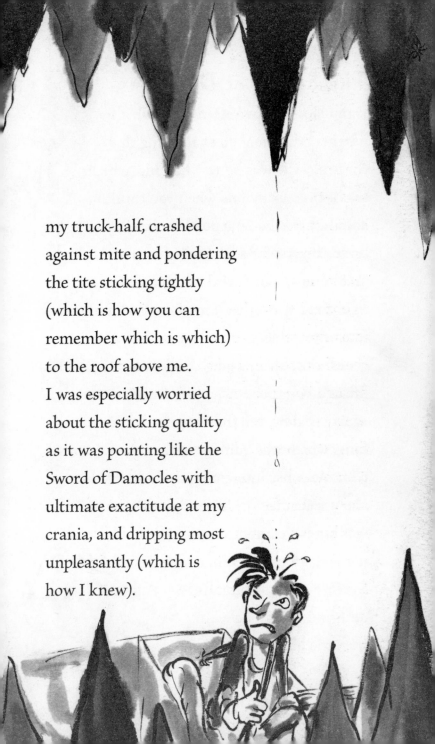

my truck-half, crashed
against mite and pondering
the tite sticking tightly
(which is how you can
remember which is which)
to the roof above me.
I was especially worried
about the sticking quality
as it was pointing like the
Sword of Damocles with
ultimate exactitude at my
crania, and dripping most
unpleasantly (which is
how I knew).

The Sword of Damocles

Damocles was an ancient Grecian moaner who moaned to the king that the king's life was better than his (which seems pretty obvious when you think about it). So the king put Damocles on his throne for a bit to shut him up and hung a large sword by a horse's hair directly overhead to make his life there uncomfortable. Damocles couldn't wait to get off the throne and go back to his regular life as a poor peasant, where he never moaned again, or, if he did, then at least not to the king, which was quite possibly His Majesty's plan. Another interesting thing about the story is that we still know who Damocles was but have forgotten the king's name. Perhaps the king forgot to remove the sword after dethroning Damocles and then the hair snapped.

What made me think about that *last* bit was
that the tite above my head had suddenly
started moving. Oh crim, I thought, and
realized that I had better suddenly start
moving myself. I yanked vigorously at
my seat belt, kicking the dashboard as
I did. Big mistake! With a noise like
a crisp bag popping, the airbag
opened and thumped me
back into my seat and pinned
me fast. Above me, my doom descended.

Doom

I have frequently read in books about people
who thought their ultimate doomitude had
arrived but then it didn't, and they later
reported seeing their life swishing like a movie
in front of their eyes. There was a man who
fell out of an aeroplane in nineteen eighty-
two and dropped seven miles through the
sky before landing in a massive pile of snow,

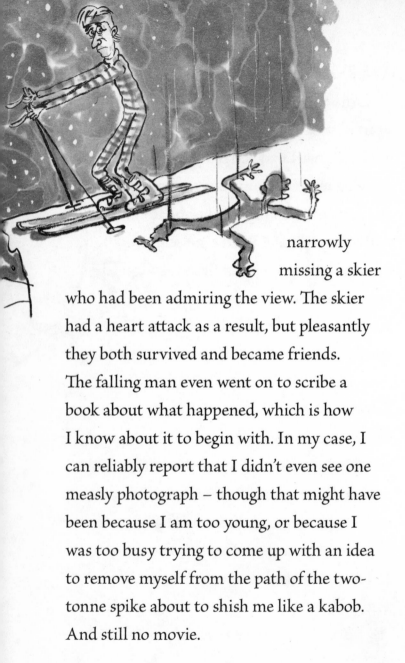

narrowly
missing a skier
who had been admiring the view. The skier
had a heart attack as a result, but pleasantly
they both survived and became friends.
The falling man even went on to scribe a
book about what happened, which is how
I know about it to begin with. In my case, I
can reliably report that I didn't even see one
measly photograph – though that might have
been because I am too young, or because I
was too busy trying to come up with an idea
to remove myself from the path of the two-
tonne spike about to shish me like a kabob.
And still no movie.

Shishkabob!

It was the shishkabob that gave me the idea. If you examine page 241 of GRANNY SAMURAI, THE MONKEY KING AND I you will see why. This is the part of that story where Granny Samurai and His Royal Simian Highness are attempting to pound each other into the earth. At a certain point in that epic battle I was able to assist by uttering a word I had learnt from Granny earlier. The word is a spell to stop time but only for a few brief seconds, and only highly locally. The word is *Sulimanasulimansalandra*. Later on my uncle made me promise never to use it again, which was fine by me. As a fan of normal life I prefer normal things happening and this does not include spells. But right now I had no choice. I opened my mouth and yelled the word out loud.

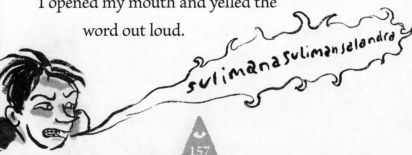

Nothing happened. That is another thing I dislike about spells. Half the time the stupid things don't work anyway.

A Spell on Spells

Once THE LOST SECRET ART OF KENJO by Granny Samurai is finished (ha ha) and is a bestseller (good luck!), Granny claims that she will publish a small book of spells for everyday usage. For example she knows a spell for making a toasted ham and cheese sandwich and another spell to make jelly set quickly instead of leaving it for hours in the fridge, and also a spell for operating the TV without a remote control.

"That's it?" I said, somewhat
surprised, as those spells
are really quite mild.
For her, anyway. She
looked at me and
shrugged.

"Also have
spell make frog
plague rain down
long time or hurricane in
envelope sign here please SURPRISE!
Plus spell to make fiery dra—"

I interrupted her flow and said hastily,
"A ham and cheese toastie is quite fine, thank
you very much."

"You think?" she said.

"I do," I replied firmly. And I did. This
of course was all later on, as right now I had
other things to worry about.

My Great Escape, and How

I stopped using my
head and decided
to use my teeth
instead.
Taking a
lesson from
the toothy
spike descending,
I bit hard into the airbag
and there was a long *pffffff* as it deflated.
I debuckled my seat belt and rolled out of
the truck JIT (Just In
Time). Two seconds
later the tite
reached my seat
and stabbed
it to the
ground.

That could have been me, I quailed innerly as I commanded my legs to start running. But two seconds is a long time for a falling thing to arrive and perhaps the spell had worked a bit after all. Then I noticed that the cave entrance was getting smaller. Weird, I thought, and, better hurry!

Then a voice I knew said, "Hello, Sam," as a red light wavered into vision. Fear singed my gizzards and I hastily commanded my legs to sprint in the other direction.

For whatever that thing was, it wasn't Philip, and wherever it was, I didn't want to be either. Like the cavalry of old I turned and charged into the caval gloom. And as I did, a fearful noise loomed up around me. It was the sound of teeth, chattering in the darkness.

Teeth

Granny Samurai has three sets of dentures, which have been specially made for her by top tooth technicians. She has her normal ones for everyday comfort and reliability. These are her stress-free teeth and are quite yellow due to considerable instant-coffee intake. She also has a set of ultra-sharp piercing teeth made decades ago by an elderly Carpathian dentist.

"Interesting," I said politely, trying not to yawn when she imparted, which means told me, that particular piece of information.

Granny grinned her yellow grin. "Is interesting," she wheezed, "if you know where Carpathia* is." Thirdly, she has a set of Old Father William titanium combat molars for – well, combat, I suppose.

163

And lastly, Granny Samurai never chatters with her teeth, only clacks. So whoever was out there noising in the darkness, it wasn't her. And where was Granny anyway? I had absolutely no idea.

* Carpathia is in Transylvania.

The Running Boy

I ran deep into the cave. The darkness was like a blanket thrown over my head and the floor beneath my feet felt soft and unpleasantly crunchy, as if I was sprinting over snails. I ran blindly, holding out one hand to fend off I knew not what. At any moment I expected a knock-out blow to be delivered by me smashing into something, or vice versa. The teeth-chattering grew louder. Behind me, a red light flashed and I glimpsed that I was running through a large tunnel.

"Sam!" shouted a tinny voice. "Sam, come back. It's me!"

Right, I thought, and accelerated. I still had an über-fresh memory of the look on Granny Samurai's face when her truck was sliced in half by the not-Philip.

"Fool me once," writes Granny in her BOOK OF AVARISMS, "shame on you. Fool me twice, watch out!"

I didn't intend on being fooled twice now if I could help it. And that was the last think I thought before the floor beneath my feet turned suddenly into a hole and I fell forwards and down.

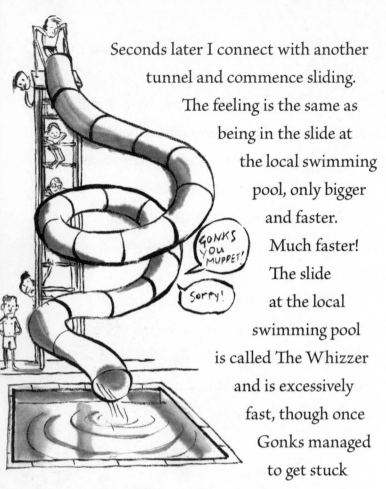

Seconds later I connect with another tunnel and commence sliding. The feeling is the same as being in the slide at the local swimming pool, only bigger and faster. Much faster! The slide at the local swimming pool is called The Whizzer and is excessively fast, though once Gonks managed to get stuck in it while Philip and I and other assorted kids piled up behind. Gonks isn't very fat or anything, he was just wearing the wrong shorts, or so he claimed.

I wished I was wearing those now.

Here I am, sliding at top
speed through the tunnel.
The walls are icky and as
slippery as soap. I am
wishing I had a light.
Here's me,
remembering that I do have
a light! I pull out my mobile
phone and switch it on.

"Do you want to reset
everything now?" spake
the irritating mobile voice
but I ignored it.

I held up my phone
as a torch and glimpsed
another hole approaching.

A second later I was
flying through it and into a space
somewhere. It was a most uncomfortable
feeling, almost as if I had just been spat.

A Spitting Interlude

Granny Samurai insists that I include the
following information in the story. She claims
to be the cherry-pit-spitting champion of
the UK – except that on one occasion she
accidentally spat her false teeth at the judges
as well as the pit, so she is banned for life.
Unfortunately she was wearing her combat
molars at the time.

Back to the Hole

Here's me, flying through the air.

The space I had been thrown into was round and vast and full of sticky filaments (which means threads). It was like being wrapped in candy floss, only the floss tasted horrible, not like delicious sugar but more like licking the dust-balls that gather under a bed. (Or so I imagined, as I had never actually licked one.) I came to a sticky stop and stared around me. This is what I saw.

yuck!

169

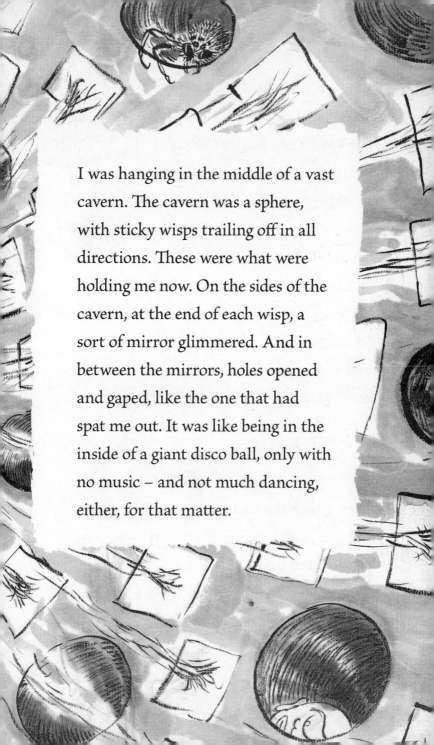

I was hanging in the middle of a vast cavern. The cavern was a sphere, with sticky wisps trailing off in all directions. These were what were holding me now. On the sides of the cavern, at the end of each wisp, a sort of mirror glimmered. And in between the mirrors, holes opened and gaped, like the one that had spat me out. It was like being in the inside of a giant disco ball, only with no music – and not much dancing, either, for that matter.

Disco Balls

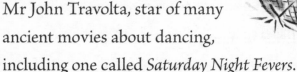

The disco ball was invented by
Mr John Travolta, star of many
ancient movies about dancing,
including one called *Saturday Night Fevers*.
The fevers were caused by lights reflecting on
the thousands of tiny mirrors glued to a ball
revolving on the ceiling and bouncing light
waves at everybody to make them dance even
more frenetically. It is a very famous device
and as Mr Travolta had a pâté on it (which
means the idea belonged to him), he became
very rich. I have never seen this movie but
I know about it because it stars on Granny
Samurai's list of the 99 Most Stupid Movies
Ever, which she will one day upload to her
website: **www.GrannySamurai.com**.

"But aren't you just making people
curious about these films," I said,
Hey!   "by writing this?"

"Exactly," she replied, and winked.

172

The Struggle Resumes

I struggled to overcome. The icky wisps were
like a hundred hands holding me. I pulled
one fist free and examined the gummy
yuck. To my high alarm my
brain activated a sudden
memory of the mat
of webby strands
hanging beneath
the skylight back at
home. It couldn't
be! I hoped fervently.
Could it? A web this size
would need millions of spiders
to create it. Wouldn't it? The thought
trembled my limbs considerably and caused
me to send violet vibrations twanging out
in all directions. This was a bit unfortunate,
actually, as spiders (if it was a web) are
highly tuned hunters who locate their prey
by exactly these means. In fact if you are

caught in a web it is a top idea to hold your breath and not to move at all. Of course this means you will eventually starve to death, but possibly that is still better than being wrapped in silken threads and injected with paralysing poison before being eaten alive. However, as these were the opposite of soothing thoughts, I reminded myself in the spirit of Uncle Vesuvio that even if some spiders showed up gnashing their teeth, they would still be much smaller than me and therefore more afraid of me than vice versa. Calmness was essential. Then the threads jerked sharply behind me and I nearly had a heart attack.

I looked around swiftly, and there, hanging not too far away, I beheld a pair of glasses – glasses that I knew.

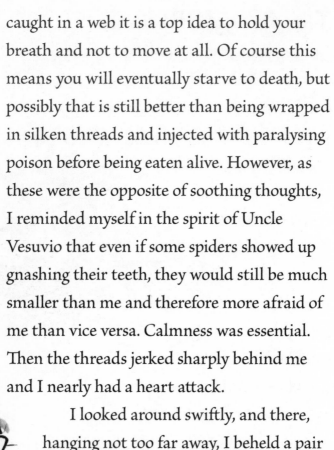

"Philip?" I said in astonishment. "Are you here somewhere?" The web stirred again and I considered the source of the stirring. Beyond the glasses, all wrapped up like a mummy of old, I could see a human-looking package of about my size.

"Philip," I said again, "is that you?" I watched in horror as a hand half forced its way out of the sticky webs and gave me a thumbs-up.

I had located my best friend.

The Thumbs-Up Sign

The thumbs-up is a trademark of Philip's, generally used by him just before everything turns into a massive disaster. Philip is a natural optimist, as is my Uncle Vesuvio. My uncle says that optimism is the first requirement for diplomatic niceties. Granny Samurai also is a natural optimist, though one who always expects the worst to happen. This is a paradox, which means two contradictory statements combining to one united thought. Granny Samurai is a paradoxical optimist. I am too young to be either.

A Sticky Rescue

I began struggling towards my best friend. "Philip," I said urgently, "I'm coming!"

The mummy-like bundle started quivering and Philip's voice said, "Sam, thank goodness! This stuff is driving me crazy." The bundle twitched as if he was trying to scratch himself but couldn't, which was of course exactly the situation.

"Don't move," I said unnecessarily. "I'm nearly there." By now I had reached his glasses and learnt that a sort of undignified doggy-paddle was the most efficient way of pushing forward through the threads.

"Sam," said Philip suddenly, "watch out for the spider."

"Ha ha," I replied with a knowing laugh, and quoting superiorly from my Uncle Vesuvio as I commenced de-wrapping Philip. "The thing is, Philip," I said, "spiders are actually much smaller than us and consequently much more scared of us than we are of them." I exposed his head as I spake this wisdom and checked his eyes at the same time.

DUCK

Blue left, green right: it was Philip all right.
I put his glasses back on his nose and he gave
me a hard Philip-look and shook his
head sadly.

"Sam," he said,
"you are a muppet."
I hesitated in my
de-wrapping.
Philip wasn't
often right,
but when he
was, *duck!*
Oh yabba,
I thought,
my eyeballs
suddenly
transfixed by an
omnibus reflection
in his glasses.
I turned my head to
behold. And I beheld.

I Spy With My Little Eye

From the other side of the web I was also being beholden – by eight nasty eyes. The eyes were black like tar blobs and bigger than grapefruits. The monstrous arachnid (i.e. spider) to which they belonged balanced lightly on the web like a hideously ugly tightrope walker. Each leg was thicker than an elephant's trunk and ended in excessively sharp-looking pincers. Its huge brown body was covered with hairs as stiff and sharp as porcupine quills (see GRANNY SAMURAI, THE MONKEY KING AND I, page 246, for further information on quillage). I could see its mouth opening and closing, and, worst of all, I could hear its inner juices blubbering. Or maybe they were mine.

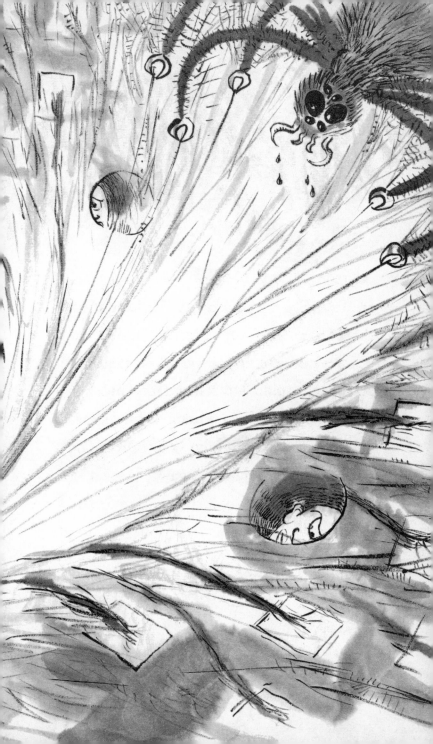

"Told you," said
Philip, then added, "and
just wait until it gets close. It stinks!"
At this the spider stuck its poison fangs
out and dripped with venomous fury. "I'M
JOKING!" shouted Philip. "I'M JOKING."
Then he emitted quickly to me, "So what's
the plan, Sam?"

Unfortunately I didn't actually have
a plan. Chapter thirty-seven of Granny
Samurai's THE LOST SECRET ART OF KENJO
deals with this situation. The chapter says,
Good luck, Patsy! And that's it.

"Patsy?" I enquisited, and
Granny grunted, "Patsy Fagan,
the man with no plan."

"What happened to him?"
I asked, and she gave a short
barking laugh.

"Everything," she
answered. I wondered
if she thought of *him*
when she went off
the bridge.

I continued unwrapping Philip. Uncle
Vesuvio recommends that even when one's
back is against the wall, one *must* continue.
Weirdly, unwrapping Philip made me think
of my birthday party again. Although it was
just yesterday, it seemed like centuries ago.
"Happy birthday to you," sang a mocking
little voice in my head, which I ignored.
Meanwhile, the spider, though hissing, still
hadn't moved to attack.

"Maybe we have a chance after all," said
Philip, and gave me another thumbs-up.
The spider charged.

This is the spider, charging. As you can
see, its legs are moving so swiftly it looks like
it has twenty of the things instead of the
usual eight. I take a deep breath and wait for
the movie of my life to start.

As I was still quite young, I didn't expect the show to last very long – which was pretty annoying if you stop to think about it. Lights. Action. Cut!

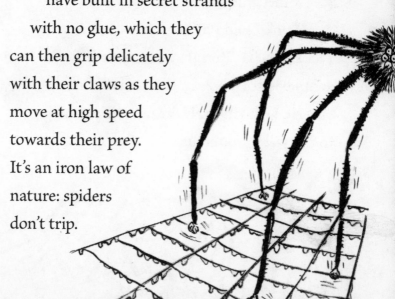

Interesting Facts About Spiders

The reason spiders don't get stuck to their own cobwebs is that they have built in secret strands with no glue, which they can then grip delicately with their claws as they move at high speed towards their prey. It's an iron law of nature: spiders don't trip.

My Movie Begins

So it was true after all. As the spider

attacked, I suddenly saw myself as a baby, in a pram with very small wheels. Or was it a shopping trolley? Anyway, I was being pushed by somebody. Then a voice shouted loudly into my movie, "DIM SUM SAM, WAKEY WAKEY!" (Or something similar.)

"Look," said Philip excitedly, and I looked. Like Tarzan, Granny Samurai swung out of a hole in the wall of the cavern. Like Cheetah she landed grinning in the webs around us.

"Boo," she announced rhetorically and hauled on some webby strands.

The spider tripped.

Arachnid Arrest

The spider flexed its claws and examined all three of us without even turning its head. You too could try this at home if you had eyes all over the place. Then the spider bent its knees (8 x 4 = 48) and did a leg shake. Now I saw why it had tripped. Granny Samurai had gathered the secret strands in her fist and tugged at just the right second.

writhe! wriggle

Grrrr!!!

Here is a law of nature about Granny Samurai: her timing is excessively excellent.

190

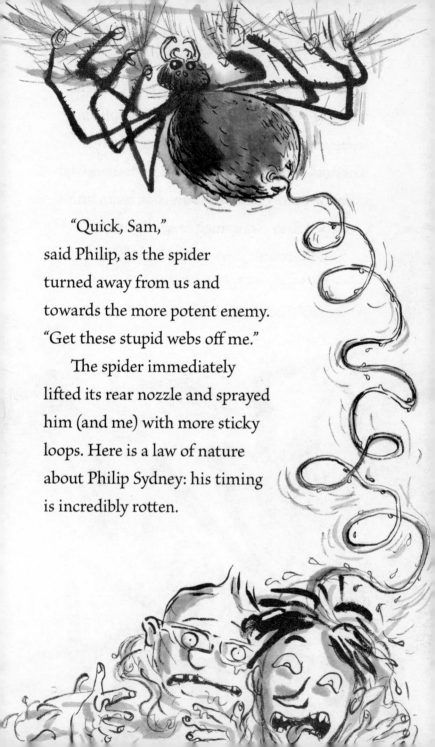

"Quick, Sam,"
said Philip, as the spider
turned away from us and
towards the more potent enemy.
"Get these stupid webs off me."

The spider immediately
lifted its rear nozzle and sprayed
him (and me) with more sticky
loops. Here is a law of nature
about Philip Sydney: his timing
is incredibly rotten.

Then a sharp twanging interrupted the
spraying. Granny had grabbed hold of some
webs and was plucking them like a banjo.
The spider hissed, its inner juices heating up.
Clearly it didn't like the banjo, or twanging
either. The twanging turned into a tune
and Granny started bawling, "INCY
WINCY SPIDER CLIMBED
UP THE WATERSPOUT."

This was another
thing the spider didn't like.
Its black blobby eyes turned a
dull throbbing red and it started
moving towards her. *"DOWN CAME
THE RAIN AND WASHED THE
SPIDER OUT!"* continued Granny Samurai
at a high scream as I hurriedly de-webbed
myself and Philip. *"OUT CAME THE SUN
AND DRIED UP ALL THE RAIN,"* she
howled. Clearly a little thing like driving
off a bridge and dropping into ultimate
nothingness hadn't affected her one little bit.
"INCY!" she roared, and the spider charged.

"*WINCY!*" she roared, though actually it was the spider who winced as its arachnid attack was met with a two-tonne Tenko-Li Tenko-La punch – enough to stop a bulldozer in its tracks and more than enough for a spider, albeit (which means even) a spider as big as a bloated rhino and twice as ugly.

"Wow,"
emitted Philip as
the excessively creepy crawly
retreated swiftly backwards into
the cobby folds of its web and hid.
Granny flexed her fist and ceased her singing.

"That's like … like…" Philip tried, and
failed, to think of a comparison.

"Like Muhammad Ali on steroids," said
Granny modestly, and a dark satisfied smirk
spread like Marmite over her face. "Don't get
old so old like me without many big tricks
up sleeve."

"Oh, I don't know," spake a voice directly behind us. "You're not *that* old, Granny. Comparatively speaking, I mean."

Comparisons of Ultimate Age

I myself am quite young, as are Philip, Meegan and Gonks. My Uncle Vesuvio is "not as young as he used to be", but who is? Granny Samurai is very ancient but won't reveal how very. From time to time I suspect that she is even older than I believe, which is very olde indeed. For example, she has a photograph in her house of the last Maharajah of Mindestan with 1879 written on it, and she is also in the picture and looks exactly the same as now.

Uncle Vesuvio says it must be her great-grandmother, but that would mean that her great-grandmother had lost a leg also, which is a very large coincidence. I am not a big believer in coincidence. And how could the voice behind us know how old she was anyway? I turned to see who was speaking, whilst a horrible premonition formed in my head. I hoped I was wrong, but unfortunately I wasn't.

"That," said Philip loudly, "is not me."

But I already knew
that. For one, I had
the real Philip before
me and had finally
finished unwrapping
him. For two, the not-
Philip was holding
a familiar-looking
lantern stick, which was
glowing with alarming
brightness. Until a loud
shot sounded and the
lantern exploded like a
firework. The not-Philip

laughed but sagged. On the other side of the
cavern Granny Samurai was already reloading
her Black
Centurion
double-action
repeater.

You can't fool Granny twice, I thought
as the not-Philip started to dissolve. Like
a snowman melting in a microwave, he
subslided back down into the tunnel.

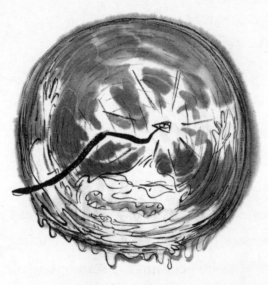

For a second the walls shimmered with
his bleared and grinning face, and then he
was gone. "Good riddance," I shouted as his
lantern stick toppled to the ground. Then far
away a drumbeat like a giant's pulse started
up. In the darkness some teeth recommenced
their chattering. Or were they mine this time?

Big Trouble in Massive Cavern

The web twanged vigorously, bouncing me back to attention.

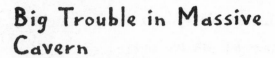

BOING!
BOI

"Oi," shouted the bouncer. "Wakey wakey Fred and Sam. They're coming."

"Who's coming?" I shouted, while Philip adjusted his glasses and looked suitably alarmed.

"Big trouble coming fast," returned Granny Samurai. "No time chitchat! Sam get moving. Find hole. Follow Fred home." She flashed her teeth like a hyena and plunged into a tunnel.

200

"Granny hold them all," she called as she vanished from sight.

SHAKE! RATTLE! ROLL!

"Is she actually enjoying herself?" muttered Philip as I turned towards him.

"No time chitchat," I quoted. "Let's go!"

"Just say the word," he replied.

"I just did," I answered.

"Right," he said. "Go where?"

"Home," I said. "Where do you think?"

"OK," said Philip, and frowned. "How, exactly?"

"BACK THE WAY YOU CAME," I frustrated loudly. "LIKE GRANNY SAID!" But fortunately Philip is a quick thinker (once he starts thinking) and almost as good at getting out of trouble as into it.

"Ahh," he said finally. "I get it. Let's go!"

Mirror, Mirror On the Wall

Philip looked quickly up and around at the walls of the cavern.

"We have to find the right mirror," he said, whilst all around the drumming and the fearsome chattering grew louder. My head felt like it was cooking in a pot of popping popcorn.

"What do you mean, the right mirror?" I asked.

Philip explained. "Those mirror things all around us are people's mirrors! And the aliens can see right through them. I think."

"What aliens?"
I asked, and Philip gave me
a look of serious impatience.

"Maybe they're not
aliens," he "explained".
"Maybe they're more like
vampires or something, though
vampires don't like mirrors, do they?
Anyway..." He took a deep breath.
"Anyway, one of those mirrors is the hole
I came in through but I have no idea which
one. And that," he added, "is a problem."

"Stop," I uttered, as the mists of confusion
started dissipating in my head. "You mean,
my *bedroom* mirror?"

"Well done, Mr Johnson," said Philip
in a sarcastic Mr Corbet voice. "That's only
what I've been trying to explain to you for
the last five minutes." I stared at Philip, who
stared back, then suddenly looked strange.

"You don't think we're dead, do you, Sam?"
he emitted uneasily. "The aliens aren't ghosts,
are they?"

"No," I said decisively, "they're not."
Because right then I knew exactly what
was going on. It was Philip's
Mr Corbet voice that had
joggled my memory. "They're
wormholes!" I uttered in
amazement. "The mirrors
are wormholes!" Now it was
Philip's turn to gape. The
gape turned swiftly to a grin.

"That's brilliant, Sam,"
he said. "Total genius! Then
it *must* be aliens," he added
in excitement. "I mean, aliens and wormholes
are like socks and smell, aren't they. You
can't have one without the other." Well, some
people can't.

Wormholes: A Primer with Diagram

Take a sharp pencil and a sheet of A4 paper and draw two dots (A + B) on opposite ends. Now draw a straight line connecting A and B. This is the shortest distance between these two points. Now fold the page so that A is exactly on top of B. Make a hole through them with the pencil. This is now the shortest distance between the two points, aka a wormhole. If this sounds easy it is only because it was discovered first by the late Albert Einstein of E = MC² fame, who made it easy for the rest of us. I wondered what advice he would give if he could see us now, then hoped sincerely that he couldn't, as that might mean that we were also late – i.e. dead – after all.

Better Late Than Never

A movement snagged my eye and jerked my head around. From one of the tunnels between the mirrors a head as big as an armchair was emerging. It had teeth that were chattering and gnashing and eyes rolling turbulently in our direction. It looked horribly happy to see us, which was not true vice versa. Then a big fist grabbed it from behind and hauled it back out of sight. Fine by me! There was the sound of a large thump, followed by a yell of Kenjo triumph.

Two seconds later
Granny Samurai lunged
her way out of the tunnel
and shook her fist at us.

"WHY STILL HERE?" she screamed.
"GRANNYWINLONGTIME
NOTALWAYS." Behind her the head
appeared again, and bit down hard on her leg.
The wooden one, I mean. Granny spun and
drop-kicked it back into darkness.

"Sam," said Philip uneasily, "look!" And
for once he didn't
mean her leg.

What he meant was that on all sides of
the cavern great gnashing disembodied
heads with rolling eyes and chattering teeth
were now extruding from the tunnels and
gumballing towards us with hostile intent.

They rolled onto the web and tumbled in our direction. They didn't seem to stick to it at all. *Gnash*, went their teeth, *gnash gnash gnash.*

"Sam," uttered Philip, "I'm really sorry I went through your bedroom mirror."

"Apology accepted," I stated. Philip looked annoyed.

"I'm not apologizing, dimbo," he said. "I'm just saying I'm sorry I went through the stupid mirror. But thanks for trying to rescue me anyway." Then a wave of anger splashed over him. "I hope you choke on us!" he shouted at the nearest approaching head. "I hope we make you sick." The head licked

its lips and grinned. It looked like it was ready to take its chances. Our end was excessively nigh. My ideas bank was totally empty. My mobile beeped.

Saved By the Beep

I pulled out my phone and looked at it. At the eleventh hour it seemed I had reception again. I pressed speed dial.

"Who are you calling?" queried Philip ironically. "The army?"

"No," I retorted. "The fire brigade!" My Uncle Vesuvio answered on the very first ring.

"Samuel," he spake, "where are you?"

"Somewhere weird!" I replied.

"Put Granny Samurai on," he said. "Immediately!"

"She's busy," I replied, then interjected swiftly, "Uncle V, no time chitchat. Open ears NOW!"

My uncle ceased speaking and opened his ears. As a diplomat he is trained to pay fast emergency attention. Also, my NOW! was loud enough to wake a hibernating bear. "We went through the mirror," I explained quickly. "I mean, Philip went through the mirror. In my bedroom. And now we can't find it again."

"I'm on my way," replied my uncle in briskly soothing tones. This is also his diplomatic speciality.

"On your way from where?" I shouted in desperation. The gnashing heads were nearly upon us, and beside me Philip was getting ready for immortal combat.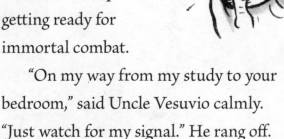

"On my way from my study to your bedroom," said Uncle Vesuvio calmly. "Just watch for my signal." He rang off.

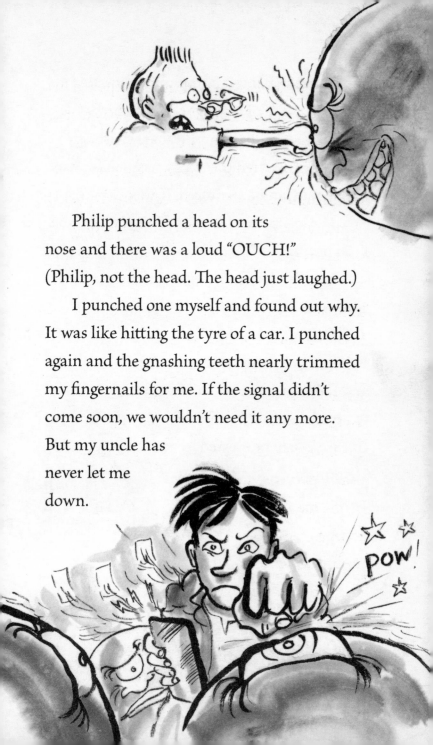

Philip punched a head on its
nose and there was a loud "OUCH!"
(Philip, not the head. The head just laughed.)

I punched one myself and found out why.
It was like hitting the tyre of a car. I punched
again and the gnashing teeth nearly trimmed
my fingernails for me. If the signal didn't
come soon, we wouldn't need it any more.
But my uncle has
never let me
down.

"There!" shouted Philip, and pointed. Directly ahead of us a light was flashing. We dodged another head and started swishing towards it through the sticky wisps. My phone rang and I answered. It was Gonks.

"Hey, Sam," said Gonks. "Are you in some kind of trouble?"

"Gonks," I said, "this is a seriously bad time to talk."

"OK," said Gonks. "It's just that I can see you in my bedroom mirror and there's a giant spider about to attack you from behind. In case you're interested."
He hung up.

Gonks

According to Philip, the most surprising thing about Gonks is that he is never surprised. Which is odd, because surprising things happen to him more than anyone else I know. For example, a pigeon once landed on Gonks's head while he was waiting at the bus stop and Gonks didn't even blink. Then he sneezed and the pigeon nearly had a heart attack. Now Gonks was apparently watching us about to be attacked from the rear by a giant arachnid and it was like he was watching a nature programme on the telly. With us as the prey.

Schon wieder!

Nature, Tooth and Raw

Here we are, fighting for our lives.

Here are the heads, also fighting for our lives but with the other meaning.

Presumably Granny Samurai is off fighting in the tunnels, because it sounds that way – i.e. loud.

And there in front of us is the signal from my uncle and the mirror to which we must get.

Around it, other mirrors were lighting up, and that's where Gonks was, too, watching as a massive spider prepared to impale us on its incisives. I should have been terrified, but right then I had more things to worry about than a stupid spider,

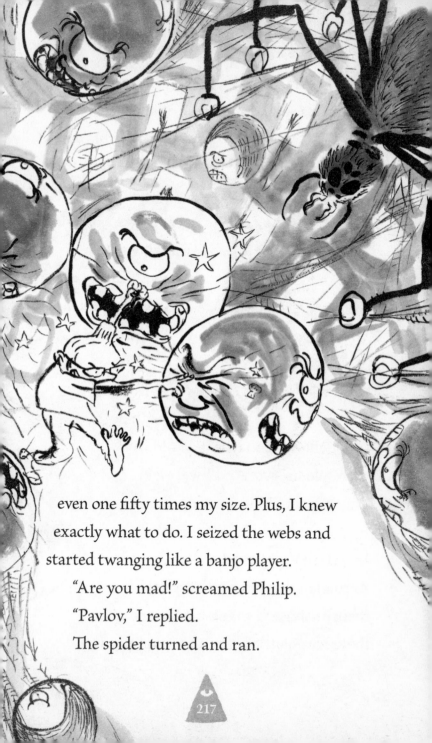

even one fifty times my size. Plus, I knew exactly what to do. I seized the webs and started twanging like a banjo player.

"Are you mad!" screamed Philip.

"Pavlov," I replied.

The spider turned and ran.

Pavlov

Pavlov was a Russian I read about in a book, who trained his dogs to associate certain sounds with certain actions, like horrible twanging with a massive Tenko-Li Tenko-La punch, for example. If it worked with dogs,

WOOF! WOOF! WOOF!

I thought, well, maybe it would work with spiders, too. And I was right.

"Wow," said Philip, impressed.

Granny Surge

Actually I was wrong, though the theory was good anyway. A second after the spider scuttled, Granny Samurai surged

218

back into the fray behind me, smiting left
and right with a large club and knocking
the giant noggins from side to side
as she advanced on us like a
Horseman of the Acropolis.
No wonder the spider
had run.

"YOU STILL HERE?" she
screamed at me, and I percepted that
it was her wooden leg she was wielding
and not a club. A giant head had bit
down hard on it and locked its jaws.

219

Its molars ground as she swung it around her head like a massively ugly toffee apple and used it to bash two comrades in quick succession. "HURRY UP!" she roared unnecessarily and shook a fist at us to encourage the following of these quite precise instructions. We hurried up.

A Mobile Interjection

By the way, intelligent readers will have already realized why my mobile suddenly worked again. Less intelligent or lazy readers may turn the book upside down for the answer.*

* On second thoughts, you can just work it out for yourselves. Here is a clue – see page 205.

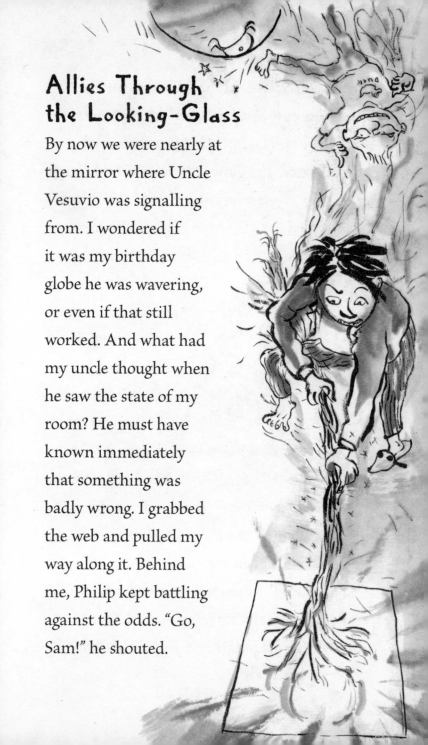

Allies Through the Looking-Glass

By now we were nearly at the mirror where Uncle Vesuvio was signalling from. I wondered if it was my birthday globe he was wavering, or even if that still worked. And what had my uncle thought when he saw the state of my room? He must have known immediately that something was badly wrong. I grabbed the web and pulled my way along it. Behind me, Philip kept battling against the odds. "Go, Sam!" he shouted.

I reached the back of my bedroom mirror. At this spot the web looked like tree roots – but glowing, as if optic fibres were buried in their insides. The glow was flowing and giving me nasty static shocks. With sudden Einsteinian insight I thought, it's energy! Energy is being sucked out of the house through the mirror! That's why my room was in decay and that's why I felt so slow and old inside it.

Behind the mirror a shape I knew knocked weakly on the glass.

"Uncle V!" I shouted, a sudden cold realization paralysing my gizzards. Then through the glass darkly my uncle lifted his

light and peered forward. Now we could see
him clearly.

"Wow," said Philip, shocked, and I fell
ultimately silent. This is why.

Uncle Vesuvio

My uncle was old and wizened. His hair was
thin and wisped, his shoulders collapsed
and hollow. He tapped on the
mirror and we could see
that it was an effort
for him even to raise
his arm. I felt sick
to think that
he had braved
the lion's den
for me. I hit
the mirror
to break it
and nothing
happened.

KNOCK!
KNOCK

"Sam stand
back NOW," rasped
a voice behind me, and to make
sure I did, the owner – i.e. Granny Samurai
– shoved me roughly to one side. "Here," she
barked at Philip, shoving her wooden leg into
his hand. "There," she shouted, turning him
around to face the giant heads that were
closing in from all sides. Clearly she
had only been able to scatter them
temporarily. My mobile rang again
and it was my uncle.

224

"Sam, you have to hurry," he whispered in a papery old man's voice.

"Keep on chitchatting nothing happen ever!" shouted Granny Samurai in a temper.

"Uncle V," I said, deeply upset, "I'm really sorry about all this." Uncle Vesuvio leant forward and placed his hand on the glass. I put my hand on his from my side.

"Cut the web, Henrietta," he instructed.

"Hello not born yesterday V," snozzled Granny Samurai in return. With one hand she reached back quickly over her head, then whisked forth a long bright sword with a curving blade and snarling dragon handle.

"Whoa, is that a samurai's sword?" asked Philip.

"Used to be," grinned Granny. "Now it's mine." She raised the sword and sliced.

Slice and Dice

The sharpest swords in the world are samurai swords. They are made by folding steel and beating it thin and folding it again and beating it thin again and doing this hundreds of times. A samurai sword is so sharp that a trained practitioner of the samurai arts can slice a hair with it lengthways.

Granny Samurai famously claims that she can shave an A4 page through

HO!

the middle and turn it into two pages. Chapter forty-six of THE LOST SECRET ART OF KENJO reveals how.

Granny writes, *Take an A4 sheet of paper. Throw it in the air. Strike on any edge and pull sword through to make two perfect A4 pages. Always remember, practice makes perfect.*

"That's not exactly telling you how to do it," I said doubtfully as I scribed this information.

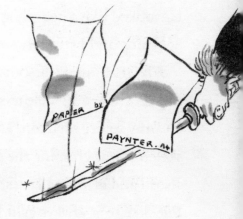

Granny looked at me piteously and said, "*Pull* Sam. Key word *pull*." She wagged her fingers at me. "And practice."

"How much practice?" I enquisited.

Granny belched and thought. "Until it hurts," she said.

Fire in the Hole

The sword struck the web at the root and stuck. The optical-fibre fibres exploded like a firework in a paint factory. The air around us was plunged into major voltic humming as if bees were swarming with electrical supremacy. Philip's hair went straight up and started smoking. He looked like a hedgehog struck by lightning and I strongly suspected I did too. In that same fearsome moment of impact I was even able to see through Granny to her skeleton. Her skeleton was gripping the samurai sword and grinning gruesomely. But skeletons always grin. Around us the heads stopped gnashing and swivelled nervously with their eyes. With a grunt, Granny twisted the sword and the web's root snapped. There was a sound like the gurgle of bathwater in a giant drain.

"Get ready," cackled Granny, and amazingly Philip just nodded and didn't ask her why or what for. The sound increased and the heads started tumbling away from us at high speed. I had a sneaking suspicion that they were moving out of range AQAP. There was a hum of pure energy. All of a sudden, Granny's topknot unravelled and her hair stood straight up on her head.

"Yikes," said Philip as a ripple of dynamic power surged out from the wormhole where it all began, i.e. my bedroom mirror. Around it, other mirrors flickered like windows lighting up in a town at night.

I caught a glimpse of Gonks, eating crisps and watching us intently from his bedroom.
Above him, Meegan Flowers had

stopped brushing her hair and was gaping as if she had just seen the oddest thing ever (which was quite possibly true). And in the mirror of Boris Hizzocks, he of Monkey King fame, Boris quivered in his bed, peeping fearfully out over his Maisy Daisy cornflower-blue duvet.

Then, with a snap like a vast biscuit breaking, my mirror opened.

"Sam…" croaked my uncle from my room, and held out an old and withered hand. But Granny was quicker.

"Visitors first," she cackled, and shoved Philip right back the way he came. She seized her wooden leg as she shoved, and I believe, although she swears she didn't, that she added a kick to his behind to speed him on his way.

"Now Sam," shouted Granny, "brace brace quick." And I girded my lions for transit. Then a stream of yellow and orange pellets whizzed past out of nowhere and hit me in the eye.

"GOTTIM!" shouted a horrid voice I knew.

"NO, I GOTTIM!" shouted an identical horrid voice. Where there are wormholes, there are worms, I thought grimly, and re-braced myself to leap. Too late! With a slurping sound, the wormholes closed and I was left to dash my head against the mirror. Ouch and mega-yabba!

233

Emergency Exit

Granny grabbed my arm and pulled me away. "Come Sam," she insisted. I went. With great uneasitude I saw that the place where she had sliced the web had started to regrow itself at top speed. The mirrors around it had faded but the air still hummed electrically.

Uh-oh, I thought as I percepted something else as well. The cavern was beginning to spin and the forces of centrifuge were descending upon us. "Tunnel quick!" roared Granny, and I followed. It was like struggling through a giant candyfloss spinner, only much less delicious. We moved around the wall as if walking on flat ground. The mirrors beneath our feet were now opaque and closed but I still avoided stepping on them. The last thing I needed was to go crashing through into *another* dimension. Finally we reached a tunnel.

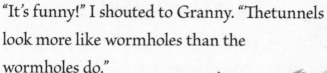

"It's funny!" I shouted to Granny. "The tunnels look more like wormholes than the wormholes do."

"Hilarious," she answered and pushed me hard. I fell, and she jumped straight after me. *Habemus exitus*, as the Romans used to say.

Back in the Whizzer

If I thought the slide in was fast,
I was wrong. For the slide out,
please imagine the slipperiest
tunnel ever, combined with
extra-frugal force from spinning,
to produce Formula 1 speeds of
ultimate felocity.

"Aaaaarrrrgggggghhhhhh!"
I yelled as I hurtled through
it, arms and legs akimbo
(which means all
over the place).

Any faster and I believe I would
have started to glow like Felix
Baumgartner, the man who
plunged to earth. Of course
he was wearing a spacesuit
and I wasn't.

Wheeee!

"AAAARRGGHHHH!"
I yelled even louder as the
tunnel whizzed me around,
with Granny Samurai
shouting "Wheeeee!"
whenever we hit a bend. My
brain was seriously considering
the possibility of blacking out when
suddenly, in one millith of the time
it took us coming in, we exited and were
flying through the air – the stale air, I might
add. And down below were the clouds and,
under those, the porridge-coloured sea.

Flying is possibly the wrong verb
to use at this point.

Falling Down

This is us, falling through the sky. Behind us is the island, spinning vigorously. Underneath me, Granny Samurai is adjusting her leg – though surely she has more important things to do, as we are dropping fast and I am a bad swimmer. In the absence of anything else to grab, I grab her. Good choice.

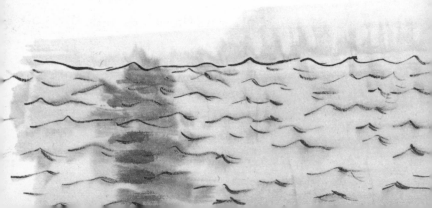

Pffffhhh! is the sound that Granny Samurai's leg makes as it goes up in smoke.

Uh-oh, I thought, before I realized that this was deliberate. Her leg concealed a NASA nano-thruster with powerful stabilizing capabilities. We spun down towards the sea, then levelled out and up as she brought it under control. Next we shot back over the waves towards the coast from whence we came.

FSSSTTTT!

240

Behind us the island stopped spinning and started to follow.

Follow?!?!?!

"WE'RE BEING FOLLOWED BY THE ISLAND!" I screamed above the rushing wind as Granny pointed her sword to slice the air and thus increase our aerodynamic efficiency. "HOW CAN AN ISLAND BE FOLLOWING US?" I shouted next, but she was either deaf or choosing to ignore me, or she knew already. We fled.

NASA
Nano-Tech

NASA is the top space agency of America, which has organized trips to the moon and lately Mars. They are very technologically superior, with a great many inventions for achieving impossible missions. I know this from reading books about them and also from their website

– www.nasa.gov – which has amazing live pictures of Mars.

"Do you know someone there?" I asked Granny Samurai later when quietude had settled back into my life.

"On Mars?" she replied.

"At NASA," I said. "Because of your top-secret nano-thruster."

"What nano-thruster?" she said, and slurped her coffee loudly.

"Forget I asked," I said.

"Asked what?" she answered. And slurped some more.

Back to Flying

The ground
below zipped
past, or rather
we zipped over
the ground below.
The ground itself
didn't move. Or maybe it
did. Suddenly I wasn't sure.
The fact is, I had the strangest
sense of shrinkage all around
me, as if the edges of everything
were closing in, and fast.

"THERE!" screamed Granny,
and pointed at the rocky coast
where the bridge had been. "NOT
FAR NOW." I glanced behind. The
island was definitely following us,
and looking angry, too. But how
can an island look angry?

I peered closer, and finally understood. It wasn't an island at all. The cave that looked like a mouth *was* a mouth. The tites that looked like teeth *were* teeth. The crater that looked like an eye socket ... *was* an eye socket. In fact the whole island was one giant head, and the cavern inside, where we had battled for our lives, must have been its brain cavity. I shivered as an eye the size of a golf green stared at me, baleful and unblinking. I pounded on Granny's arm to go faster.

"Three seconds to touchdown," she replied as the ground came up to meet us. Actually, it was only one.

Landing

This is us, "landing". As you can see, we are saved by the drifts of ash that lie around and taste as horrible as ever.

I struggled to my feet and beheld the tracks of Granny's truck before us. I realized that we were back exactly where we had started. Well, nearly. Like an angry rising sun in the sky above us, the head loomed.

The Breath of Death

"The drawing, Sam get ready!" shouted
Granny Samurai, and shoved the paper
towards me. I grabbed it as she whirled
to face our enemy. I held it up and looked
around for our exit. *The fire is dying,*
I glimpsed, *and I can
hear their teeth rattling
in the darkness.* I gritted
my teeth and looked
around for our exit.

Above us the head opened
its mouth and started to inhale.
My hairs commenced lift-off.

"HURRY SAM HURRY!" roared
Granny unnecessarily as ashy particles
whirled up through the air around
us. Her legs were bent and she
wielded her sword at exactly the

correct angle for supreme Kenjo cutting (47°).
Her other hand had twisted into an eagle's
claw and I knew she was preparing to inflict
upon our enemy her full Silent Shriek
of Animalistic Annihilation.
I interrupted quickly.
"Granny Samurai,"
I urged, "before you
commence with
shrieking, I can't
find our exit…"
The shriek
commenced.

A Shriek in Time

Granny shrieked. The head inhaled. The air around me thickened as ashy particles were whisked into a frenzy then sucked up into the vast mouth above. Any second now and I would follow, like a mouse sucked into a Dyson. I peered wildly through the flying debris for any sign of a wormhole. Then the Silent Shriek of Animalistic Annihilation peaked and a smudge of light wobbled in the air before me.

I had found it!

Remembrance of Spells Past

I held up the paper and decanted, *"Inkibus minkibus succubus omnibus.* Er … *Poopla hoopla moopla."* The head kept hoovering. *"INKIBUS MINKIBUS SUCCUBUS OMNIBUS. POOPLA HOOPLA MOOPLA,"* I repeated, more loudly now, and a fiery dot appeared in the centre of the smudge before me. By now my feet had lifted from the ground and were pointing towards the "cave", i.e. the mouth. I gripped Granny's coat and held on. *"INKIBUS MINKIBUS SUCCUBUS OMNI..."* I bellowed for the third time, and the page tore from my hand and whirled up and into the giant mouth, all except for a fragment still pinched between my thumb and finger. With a sound like a bank vault shutting,

the vast
mouth closed
and the fiery
dot died in the
air before me.
The inhalation
ceased and
I returned
suddenly and
painfully, knees-first,
to the ground.

"Ouch," I uttered. The big head grinned.

Grinning

Interestingly, human beings are the only

animals that grin. If you grin at a
monkey it will think that you
are showing it your teeth as
a prelivery to attack, so
watch out. When Granny
Samurai grins it may also

250

be a prelivery to attack, so watch out also.
But most menacing of all grins I have known
was the one on the giant head above us then.
That and the glimpsing of the tites and mites
jabbing and dangling on the inside. Worse,
those toothy deformations were now not
only grinning but also engaged in eating our
only way out of this ashy dimension – i.e. the
drawing. Multo-yabba from me and no grins
either, I can reliably inform you.

Gripping

But Granny wasn't grinning either. Instead
she held her sword aloft and ready, like a
warrior of old. "Don't panic," she uttered,
which normally would have made me panic
considerably.

Instead I replied calmly, "I am beyond
panic," and as I spake, I thought perhaps I do
have diplomatic tendencies after all, and later
on might follow in the footsteps of my uncle

instead of becoming a highly paid scientist.
(Assuming there was a later on, of course.)
"At least we rescued Philip," I continued quite
proudly.

"Who?" said Granny Samurai.

"Fred," I answered, and she muttered
something rude under her breath. Above us
the head had finished chewing and was now
contemplating us fiercely. A zit appeared
over its eye, then travelled down its face and
mouth and out onto its tongue, becoming
more and more like somebody I knew in
the process, somebody like Granny Samurai
but a bipedal version, which means
with two whole legs.

"That not me," said Granny unnecessarily, but I barely heard her. My attention was consumed by the red lantern on a stick that the not-Granny was holding in her hand. My calmness retreated like the tide. The real Granny growled and blinked her eyes slowly one after another like a kimono dragon.

The hour of our ultimate doomitude had finally arrived.

Famous Last Words

As a scribe I am quite interested in famous last words. For example, there was a man who uttered his famous last words but then didn't decease for two whole weeks, during which time he was utterly silent as he wanted his famous last words to be just that. What they were I have forgotten. Then there was King George, who motioned all his courtiers and royal family closer before saying "BOO!", then died, which was quite pithy and amusing also. And now there was me. I didn't have any last words, nor did I want any, but I thought I should write an excessively fast note to my uncle saying goodbye and thanking him for looking after me all these years. I took out my moleskin notebook.

Dear Uncle Vesuvio, I scribed quickly, then stopped, and flipped back a page. "Ahhh, Sam, you *muppet!*" I uttered to myself as I beheld what I had completely forgotten. It was my copy of the drawing and spell. "Look," I said to Granny, and it was the first time I have ever seen her surprised.

"Well done Sam muppet!" she roared. "Now HURRY!" And I hurried. The not-Granny swiped its red lantern down hard.

The Art of Swordplay

Chapter seventy-one of
THE LOST SECRET ART OF
KENJO deals with swordplay.
Swordplay, writes Granny
Samurai, *is about seeing
all the angles. Quickly!*

I thought of
this now as a blade
of blue light cracked like
lightning towards us.

But Granny Samurai was faster.
With infinite precision she moved the
angle of her sword just 0.2 millimetres,
caught it on the tip and deflected it.

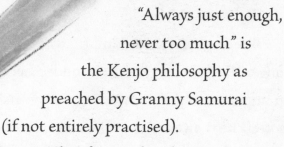

"Always just enough,
never too much" is
the Kenjo philosophy as
preached by Granny Samurai
(if not entirely practised).

Our attacker frowned and swiped
again, harder this time. Granny dropped
her sword two centimetres and
deflected once again.

By now I had
completed the
second chant and
a hole was starting
to open in the
wobble of light
before me. Come
on, I thought.
Come on!!

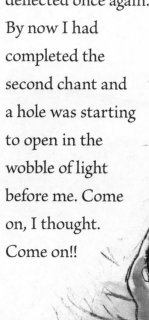

Beside me Granny Samurai was no longer thinking but had surrounded herself in impenetrable concentration. Above us the not-Granny swelled horribly and sprouted spider legs. It seemed to be quite annoyed at the turn of events. With a massive *schwip* (swipe plus dip) it slashed the blue light at us for the third and fiercest time, the Breath of Death starting up again

as it did so. Granny Samurai caught
this flash on the flat of the blade and,
instead of deflection, twisted her wrist with
a powerful flick to bounce it back against
her foe. The lantern bloomed with light and
splintered.

"INKIBUS MINKIBUS SUCCUBUS,"
I roared for the grand finale, and with a
woomph! a hole opened in the firmament

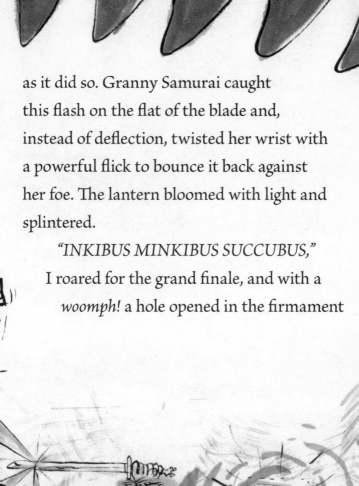

before us and
I could suddenly
see right through to the
main street of our home town. It was early
morn outside, and bright and welcoming.

"Come on, Granny Samurai!" I shouted,
and jumped. As I jumped I grabbed her fur
and hauled her with me. Most of her, anyway.
Behind us came a howl of rage and with a
noise of ultimate Mister Slush slurpitude,

the wormhole closed, neatly chopping off the
end of her wooden leg as it did so.

"Yabba," muttered Granny, then
checked the rest of her and cheered
up quickly. "Megawocka Sam,"
she said and clapped me
painfully on the back.

263

We lay sprawled on the pavement just outside the International Bank of BizCom Ltd. I could see by our reflection in the window that we were an excessively sorry-looking sight, but I didn't care. We were still alive.

A passer-by glared at Granny and said, "You should be ashamed of yourself, letting a poor child beg like that," and Granny started laughing. I might have laughed myself if memory hadn't suddenly intruded.

"Uncle Vesuvio!" I shouted, and jumped to
my feet to hail a taxi. One stopped and
the driver gave us a look but
Granny gave him a look
and he opened the door.
"Number 5 Summerhill
Road!" I shouted, and
off we sped, AQAP
of course.

screech!!!

Home Sweet Home

We pulled into my road and screeched to a stop. Summerhill Road is a pleasant road with houses and trees on it. Numbers 4, 6 and 7 were OK, but my house, number 5, was a terrible mess. The roof was sagging and the chimney had collapsed. The windows looked like broken teeth and the hedge was weedy and overgrown.

"Are you sure this is the right address?" asked the driver doubtfully. "It doesn't look like anyone has lived here in years."

"Tsk tsk modern materials," Granny commented as she paid him. Meanwhile I had exited the car at top speed with emergency shouting.

"Uncle Vesuvio…!" I called. "Uncle Vesuvio!" I shoved at the rusty garden gate and it broke in my hand. My heart was beating hard.

Then, just inside the gate, a voice said, "Hello, Samuel," and stopped me in my tracks. It was my uncle, thinner and weaker than usual but a million times better than when I saw him last. I ran and hugged him, knocking him over as I did so (by accident of course). "Careful, Samuel," he said, "I'm still not completely recovered. My legs are a bit shaky." I hugged him again. Behind us Granny Samurai hopped into the garden on one leg, not shaky at all and

268

grinning widely. My uncle looked at her and she held up a finger.

"Not my fault V. Big rescue no time think just act."

My uncle smiled. "I was going to say thank you, Henrietta," he emitted.

"No biggie," she replied, and winked. At me, I mean, not my uncle.

"And thanks to Philip, too," my uncle went on. "He was the one who dragged me out of the bedroom before it was too late. It's funny," he amended. "I was expecting you to come through the wormhole, Samuel, but then Philip appeared instead."

"Typical," I said, and laughed, and hugged my uncle again. If anything had happened to him I might have had to go and live with

Granny Samurai, which might be interesting
but frankly also a bit alarming.

"Where is Fred anyway?" asked Granny,
and just then Philip came running
around the corner.

"Sam!"
he shouted. "You're back!"
Behind him, Gonks and Meegan were in tow,

with David Curley also, and Michael Finn and Wowser. They were all armed to the teeth – except for Wowser, of course, who had his own.

"We were just coming to rescue you," gasped Philip.

"Through the mirror," said Gonks, slapping one hand with his hammer. "Ouch," he added.

Meegan said, "What's going on, Sam? Philip tried to explain but I can't understand what he's on about."

I hesitated and looked at Granny Samurai, who shrugged, then at Uncle Vesuvio, who considered, then said, "Well, Samuel, why don't you invite everyone inside and I'll make us a nice cup of tea while you explain."

And so we did.

Both, I mean.

And ate biscuits

whilst explaining.

No Further Explanation Necessary

I not only told my
friends exactly
what had happened,
I didn't even swear
them to secrecy –
because a) nobody would
believe them anyway, and

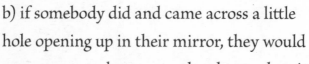

b) if somebody did and came across a little
hole opening up in their mirror, they would
know exactly what to do – i.e.
run. Away, I mean. Fast!
And one week later, at
the request of my uncle,
who had by then fully
recovered, I sat down and
scribed out everything
that had happened into
my moleskin notebook
and presented it to him.

"What will you do with it?" I asked.

"I shall put it away carefully in my study."

"More carefully than the last time?" I replied. And my uncle laughed.

"Much more carefully," he emphasized, then hesitated. "But some things want to be found," he said. "It doesn't matter how well you hide them, they just wait until the right person comes along. Or the wrong one," he added, which gave me the shivers slightly.

"Did you find those pages once too?" I asked then casually.

Uncle Vesuvio paused and looked at me carefully.

"No," he replied. "I wrote them."

Epilogue

An epilogue is stuff that happens after a story is over. This is the epilogue to this story, one month later.

Drooone

Now that the wormhole interlude had subsided, life resumed normality. Philip started working on a comic about a master thief who uses wormholes to steal alien artefacts from other dimensions. "But you're the one who's always telling us to write about what we know," he complained when Mr Corbet

found him working
on it during class, and
confiscated it. And
Gonks has a new pet,
which he claims appeared
in his room while all that weirdness was going
on. It looks suspiciously like the hamfrog as
presented to me by Granny Samurai but hairy
again and less shrunken. Gonks calls it "Olm"
and he is welcome to it if it is.

The horrible neighbours came over and
moaned about the state of our house and
garden and threatened to move if we
didn't do anything about it,

so my Uncle
Vesuvio told
me to freeze all
home improvements
until further notice.
(Except for the inside,
of course, as we are
both tidy people and
dislike living in a mess.)
In fact the first thing
I did was to de-cobweb
the skylight and chase the
spiders away, which was excessively easy after
everything I had just been through.

276

"*Incy Wincy Spider,*" crooned Granny when I told her, slurping her cold instant coffee and burping loudly. It had been a week since her last visit and she was looking quite pleased with herself.

"Is that a new leg?" I asked, as now she had a wooden one back on, which looked very much like the old one.

"Old leg new, new leg old," she replied mysteriously, and cackled and slurped again. I frowned with forbearance (which means patience + irritation).

"So it *is* your old leg?" I pursued, while she ate some sugar from the bowl and grinned knowingly. "How did you get it back?"

"Sam worse than Fred. Who what why blah blah blah leg leg leg!" She squished some coffee through her teeth cracks and gave me a dark look. "I went and asked nicely," she said primly. "If you really want to know."

"Oh really?" I replied.

"Yes really," she echoed and made a noise like a gorilla eating a whoopee cushion.

I desisted from further questioning.

And Finally...

I have one last
thing to scribe.
Actually I have
not scribed this
per se, but copied
it from a book
that I found in
my uncle's study
at the beginning
of this story. The

alert reader will remember that one book
was called LOST WORLDS AND THEIR
SUSPECTED LOCATIONS, WITH MAPS AND
SHIPPING TIMETABLES. Towards the end of
that book is a chapter called "Mythical
Worldes of Olde", which I went back to and
studied carefully. In that chapter I found
the following pages, scribed by an unknown
traveller from 1703, which is very ancient by
nearly all standards.

I magine, Gentle Reader, what Horror I behelde, when my Doome appeared above me as a Hideous HEAD of greate Size, as of a Mountain, with gaping Jawes and Teethe to crushe and engulfe me.

FIG 1. THE FLOATING WORLD

13

280

This BRAINE of ULTIMATE DOOMITUDE, a floatinge Worlde which does appear at Intervals between the celestial Spaces of this Planete and the Nexte, is malevolante and darke of Beinge, committed to devouring and destroying of our Life's Source and Energies. Therefore let the DOORES of HEAVEN be barred and locked for all Time and sette with Charms of Hindrance that this Destroyer may knocke yette not enter, and having knocked, pass on; nor may we feel its wicked Breath upon us, or see its baleful Gaze. I write this, in the Yeare of 1703.

And then a bit has been torn out of the book, so we may never know who wrote it, which is maybe just as well.

"But that's what I said. Basically," uttered
Philip when I showed him what I had found.
"On that day in class with Mr Corbet,
remember?" Well, I did remember, and as
I previously remarked about Philip Sydney,
he's mostly wrong about everything, but when
he's right, he's mega-right. On the other hand,
as my uncle sometimes observes, anybody can
be right by accident.

Over and Out

The story is now officially over. Alert readers may have also spotted that the drawing on the inside cover is almost identical to the one that opened up the door to another dimension. However, there are several small changes so that it won't work at home. This is for extra-legal reasons, as otherwise some readers might be tempted to try it for themselves. I don't recommend the experience. Goodbye.

Samuel Johnson Esq

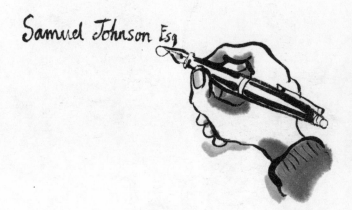

This is the first book starring
Sam and Granny Samurai.
Granny says, "Read it NOW."

← (The
Monkey King)

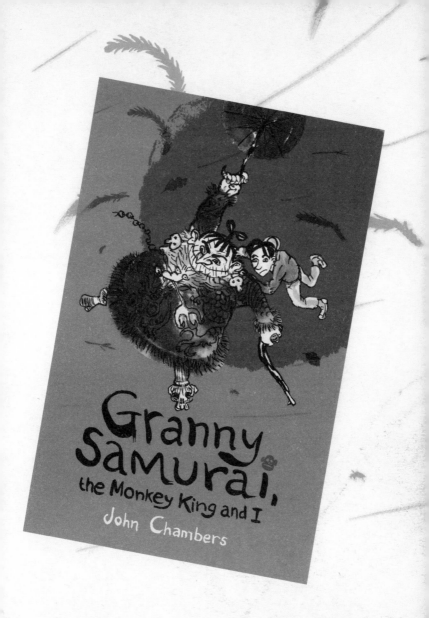

Granny Samurai,
the Monkey King and I
John Chambers

"A wonderful, original comedy." *Inis*

John Chambers was born and raised in Ireland and grew up near the sea. He writes and draws for a living. Once, when he was younger, he won a colouring competition and received an Action Man with real "eagle" eyes as a prize. Maybe if he had won a maths contest he would be an accountant today. He has three children and they can all draw very well.

Samuel Johnson lives and scribes in the UK. He is still considering what he will do when he grows up.